As Gutt advanced, Holt took two more steps backward. He reached automatically for his gun, then remembered it was in the marshal's belt.

Gutt stood between him and Pert's inert form, no more than ten yards distant. "What did I tell you in Utah?"

"I told you I am brutal by nature," Gutt reminded Holt. As if in confirmation, Gutt bent over the unconscious Pert and Holt thought he meant to break the U.S. marshal's neck. But Gutt only rifled Pert's pockets until he found the key to the manacles.

"I told you I would kill you if you persisted in harassing me." Gutt unlocked one cuff, then the other. "Now I shall."

Gutt advanced slowly, and then suddenly he was upon Holt. The huge man grabbed at Holt's shoulder and rode him down into the snow. His bulk pressed the breath from Holt's lungs.

Gutt clamped his huge hands around Holt's neck. . . .

Also by Steven M. Krauzer:
Published by Fawcett Books:

GOD'S COUNTRY

WINTER OF THE WOLF

Steven M. Krauzer

FAWCETT GOLD MEDAL • NEW YORK

Sale of this book without a front cover may be unauthorized. If this book is coverless, it may have been reported to the publisher as "unsold or destroyed" and neither the author nor the publisher may have received payment for it.

A Fawcett Gold Medal Book
Published by Ballantine Books
Copyright © 1994 by Steven M. Krauzer

All rights reserved under International and Pan-American Copyright Conventions. Published in the United States of America by Ballantine Books, a division of Random House, Inc., New York, and simultaneously in Canada by Random House of Canada Limited, Toronto.

Library of Congress Catalog Card Number: 94-94034

ISBN 0-449-14869-6

Manufactured in the United States of America

First Edition: June 1994

10 9 8 7 6 5 4 3 2 1

For Dorrit

Chapter One

It was fascinating, Holt thought, how many notions could pass through your mind in the span of eight seconds: the abstraction that you wished to be anywhere else at this moment; the observation that you could hold no solid image in your field of vision, only lantern-show-like snapshots of sky, hard-packed ground, faces of men who perched on a fence rail, your own hand cinch-wrapped at the base of a horse's mane; the anticipation of at any moment getting your neck broke.

While Holt's brain was elsewhere, his legs were automatically pumping, his spur rowels raking and gouging at the animal's withers. The horse's reaction was reasonable enough: It was doing everything instinct could devise to throw Holt off its back.

The bronco sunfished, arching the half ton of its body into a bow. All four hooves left the ground for a moment, and then it came down hard on the front pair. Holt was thrown forward so violently he almost banged his nose on the horse's hide. He jerked himself upright as the animal went into a twirl. It didn't appear to be losing any of its energy; that made one of them, Holt reckoned.

The horse reared, landing with a jolt so profoundly spine-compressing that Holt expected when this was over, he'd be six inches shorter. But he went on raking as the horse feinted another buck and instead tried to toss him sidewise, as if it actually had any sense. Holt hung on, and a moment later blessedly heard the shrill whistle that meant his eight seconds had elapsed.

He heard the encouraging hoots and hollers of the cowboys on the fence; during the ride, his world seemed drained of sound, in the way a dream is sometimes absent of colors. But now that he'd managed to stay aboard for the time required to qualify his ride, he was faced with the issue of dismounting.

That Holt was no longer scraping with his spurs did little to mollify the bronco. It bucked on with undiminished vigor, as if this were now a personal conflict. Holt looked for a propitious moment to let go of the cinch with some chance of landing on a nonvital part of his anatomy.

The horse abruptly abandoned its antics and took off in a pure straight gallop at the nearest fence rail. Holt had grown up with horses, and knew this one would stop—probably. In a similar circumstance, he'd once seen a horse die of a massive heart attack but continue running on pure nervous-system mechanics, crashing right through a corral's plank wall.

But this one stopped after all, swinging sideways at the last moment and slamming its rump against the rails. Holt heard one break as he was thrown ass-over-teakettle above the fence top. He did a complete flip and landed flat on his butt.

The horse snorted and sprayed him with flecks of spittle, then trotted away docilely. Holt thought he might just sit there for long enough to inventory his skeletal parts, but by and by Teddy Brantville was standing over him extending his hand, so to save face Holt had to take hold and let Brantville pull him to his feet. He was relieved to find he was able.

"A fine ride, Mr. Johnson," Brantville intoned. The cowboys were gathered around, and one slapped Holt on the shoulder. It was meant in bonhomie, but it made his spine jerk with a spasm of pain.

Brantville ticked off a mark in his notebook. "I score it at eighty-three. You have won second place."

"What do you have to do to win first?" Holt inquired. "Pick up the horse and toss him over the barn?" But the mark was fair; earlier Holt watched while a rider named Mars endured an equally aggressive animal, and with somewhat more grace.

Brantville laughed pleasantly. On the edge of the ring of cowhands, Holt saw Samantha Lowell. The boys weren't sure what their relationship was, but they were polite enough not to ask questions, and treated her with courtesy. Now they parted to admit her.

Sam looked him over, nodding as if satisfied that he was still alive. She gestured with her chin toward the rails over which Holt had been tossed.

"Don't ever take up boxing," she advised. "You just got thrown out of the ring."

The rodeo was partly sport and partly the breaking of horses, and the centerpiece of the activities marking the end of the fall roundup on Teddy Brantville's spread, thirty miles south of the Missouri River Breaks. The first day of November had dawned that morning on the rolling plains of central Montana, and the next day the cowhands who'd served Brantville through the summer of stock growing would be riding out for who knew where. Most would return the next season; those who found better wages or new professions or, once in a while, violent death, would never be heard from again.

"Which way are we heading?" Sam said at Holt's side.

Now and again she demonstrated a disconcerting facility for reading Holt's thoughts, but he'd learned to live with it. She was good company, a steadfast partner in all ways, and a handsome companion to boot. Somewhere in her late twenties, perhaps ten years Holt's junior, she had a trim, compact figure, full lips, and high, slightly freckled cheekbones. She was dressed at the moment like most of the men, in flannel shirt, leather jacket, and denim jeans with the cuffs rolled above riding boots.

"You decide," he said. "We been here the better part of two months, so we're following a cold trail."

"No trail at all," she amended.

It was evening, and the end-of-season festivities continued with Brantville hosting an outdoor banquet. He'd ordered one of his fat beeves butchered, and a hindquarter was roasting on a spit over a big pit fire dug in upwind from the corrals and barn near the ranch's main house, a two-story frame structure that looked like it got a fresh coat of whitewash every spring. Brantville was a widower of middle years who lived with his cows, horses, and housekeeper, a hawk-nosed, spare, wire-haired biddy named Eliza Maplethorn.

Mrs. Maplethorn brooked no nonsense from these boys, not that nonsense was frequently offered. Brantville's hands might be semidrifters, but like Holt, they came from what passed for middle-class backgrounds, had some schooling, and adhered to a code that was basically grounded on courtesy and getting along. None was armed; their handguns were tools worn only on the job, for dispatching the occasional injured horse or cow, or a predatory wolf. The Brantville ranch was a place of serene industry, and in many ways, even as Holt was itching to get moving again, he appreciated the time he and Sam had been afforded here.

The oldest of the hands rotated the spit of beef and poked at it with a long steel fork. "Just about ready, Eliza," he hollered. "Better see to the potatoes."

On the front porch of the big house, Mrs. Maplethorn placed her hands on her hips and thrust out her bony chin. "That's Miz Eliza," she declared.

"I'm near as old as you." That brought some chuckles from the crowd. "I guess I can dispense with the 'Miz.'" Aside from some desultory herding, this man's main job was helping to feed the crew. He liked to talk in his off hours, and Holt didn't mind listening, so he knew the oldtimer had worked as provisioner on innumerable wagon trains in his early days. Inevitably, that meant he was known to one and all as "Cookie."

Mrs. Maplethorn put aside her mostly feigned pique and went inside for the spuds, while Cookie basted the meat with red sauce. Though the days were growing shorter, this one had been bright and clear, and the sun was still an hour above the peaks of the Rocky Mountain Front, sixty miles off to the west. "In a way I'm sorry to leave, too," Sam said to Holt. Her arm brushed his.

"We got ourselves a little grubstake," Holt said. "Near a hundred between us, plus the twenty-five I won this afternoon." His back spasmed a bit. "Damn that bronco. I think he had some personal grudge."

"You're feeling abashed." Now she touched at his arm. "Would it help if I said I was concerned for you?"

Holt looked at her. "Were you?"

Sam gave him a roguish smile. "Why, I don't know," she said. "I hadn't considered until this moment."

Nearby a cow lowed. Mrs. Maplethorn came out of the house with a caldron of boiled potatoes, and went back for stewed carrots and fried tomatoes. The dozen or so men lined up for their plates. Cookie said something admonishing about manners, and the first man in the queue deferred to Sam, who graciously accepted his place.

Cookie had some culinary talent, and Mrs. Maplethorn was no mean hand herself. The beefsteaks were tender, well-sauced, and, most important to Holt, generously cut; nearly getting one's back broken did wonders for the appetite. Mrs. Maplethorn insisted that Brantville keep a few milk cows, so the potatoes were flavored with butter, and although Holt didn't have much truck with vegetables, he was hungry enough to down a portion of carrots and tomatoes as well. He forked up the last square of his second slice of beef and enjoyed a satisfying belch, which earned him a look from Sam.

"You got that right," he said languidly. "I could enjoy this." He was even entertaining the notion of lolling back for a postprandial nap, when Brantville appeared before the bench on which he and Sam were sitting.

"Are you finished, Mr. Johnson?"

Over the weeks here, Holt had always been disconcerted with the formality, probably a result of giving the kindly rancher a false name. "That was a real fine feed, Mr. Brantville," he said.

"It is time to settle accounts," Brantville said. The previous day, he and Holt had ridden down to a middling-sized village called Lewistown, where they'd passed the better part of the day while Brantville withdrew two thousand dollars in cash from the First Territorial Bank. Brantville said he wished some company for the twenty-mile round trip, but Holt suspected there was more to it than that. Brantville struck him as an astute judge of character, and Holt figured the rancher had recognized that in case of predation, Holt knew which end of a revolver was which. But they went unmolested as they transported the sack of cash, discussing the weather and the fine country and the market for beef and similar matters of little consequence.

"My custom is to have a private word with each of my people when I pay the wages." Brantville looked around and lowered his voice, in a way that increased Holt's disconcertment. "Our talk might take a bit longer, so you two will visit with me last."

"Yes sir," Holt said. He watched Brantville approach the hand named Mars, who'd won the rodeo prize, and the two of them went inside the big house.

Holt sat back down, got out his makings and began work on a cigarette. "You think he suspects?" Holt licked at the paper.

Sam accepted the cigarette. "I think he's known from the start."

Holt turned ideas over while he built a second smoke. "But he didn't make an issue of the matter. That means we're not in trouble."

Sam exhaled smoke. "Not from him, I'd warrant," she said, "but generally speaking, we've been in trouble since the day we met."

CHAPTER TWO

Teddy Brantville's office was the first chamber to the left of the entryway hall, a spacious room furnished with a sideboard and two armchairs facing a broad flat-topped desk. On it was a leather-edged blotter, a pen and inkwell, goosenecked lamp, and in one corner, a three-inch-high stack of foolscap paper with writing on the top sheet that Holt recognized as Sam's hand. Large mullioned windows looking south and west provided a panoramic view of the rancher's domain, and around the sashes the walls were covered with red-and-white flocked paper. Sam gazed out, watched the men passing the three bottles of whiskey that Brantville had provided, enough to make them mellow without causing liquor-driven hijinks. Cigarette tips winked in the gathering twilight.

Behind Holt Brantville said, "Did you have a drink?"

Holt turned. One of the interior walls framed a stone fireplace where cottonwood chunks blazed against the chill of the autumn night. Around it, towering above the desk and framing the door of the adjacent wall, were shelves running floor to ceiling, filled with what had to be thousands of books. Outside of a Carnegie library, Holt had never seen so many volumes in one place. "I took a taste," Holt answered.

Brantville gestured them into the chairs and went to the sideboard, where amber whiskey in a crystal decanter sat amidst matching glasses. He smiled, not unkindly. "Another, perhaps? To settle the nerves, as they say."

Holt shook his head politely and watched Brantville

pour. The stockman was tall and lean, and looked to be maybe in his mid-fifties. His full head of mostly dark hair was cropped short and, like his handlebar mustache, flecked with streaks of white. He wore gabardine trousers over pointy-toed, high-heeled riding boots that had been recently polished, a white linen shirt, and a suede vest.

Sam accepted a glass from Brantville and thanked him. Brantville took his own drink to the desk and perched himself beside the pile of paper, tapped absently at it. "I want no doubts to linger once you have left," Brantville said.

Given the crack about nerves, Holt assumed Brantville was talking about their secrets, his and Sam's. But the rancher's demeanor was jovial rather than threatening, and to Holt's relief, he continued, "Surely you wondered what your partner and I were doing all that time you were seeing to my livestock."

"I mind my business," Holt said neutrally, "and Sam didn't volunteer to me any of yours."

Brantville nodded, as if that was a good answer. "When I came into this territory in 1854, there were perhaps five dozen Europeans in all of Montana, mostly clustered southwest, in the Bitterroot Valley. There I settled, first to trade with the Flathead Indians and later to begin my initial herd."

"If you were still there five years later, we were almost neighbors," Holt said. "My people ranched in the Beaverhead."

Brantville was surprised. "Are they still there?"

"My father was killed in a riding accident while I was in the war." To Brantville's inquisitive reaction, Holt replied, "On the Union side. Anyway, we sold out and my mother went back East."

Sam shook her head slightly, as if giving him permission to omit the details of the minié ball he'd taken a fraction of an inch from his spine, the bullet that had nearly crippled him and left him shy of getting shot ever since. To switch the conversation from himself back to Brantville, Holt said,

"You hired Sam to do your accounts, is all I know. I reckon she was good at it."

Brantville bowed slightly at Sam. "Indeed, but my accounts hardly take more than a few days each month." Brantville tasted his drink. "I have seen and done some things," he said formally.

"In the early sixties, I drove my dozen head of cows to Virginia City soon after gold was struck," Brantville went on. "I provided beef for the miners, ran a mercantile, prospected a bit myself, with no particular success. When Henry Plummer visited his depredations on the camp, I helped—" Brantville searched for the right words. "—put an end to his shenanigans."

Holt knew of the notorious Plummer. At the same time he served as sheriff, he was also running a band of road agents that committed the most outrageous robberies and murders. The citizens of the mining district finally reached the end of their rope, and so did Plummer. Along with dozens of his men, he was hanged in the early days of 1864 by vigilantes. Apparently Brantville was among them.

"During the seventies," Brantville said, "I was elected to three terms in the Territorial Legislature, while building up what you see here. Adventures ensued—conflict with rustlers, peace with the Indians, political intrigues, and the like."

Brantville waved a hand to take in the shelves that surrounded them. "And I built my collection. Once, in the early times, I heard that a band of emigrants had gone bust near Deer Lodge, and possessed books now for sale. I rode two hundred miles round trip to purchase five tomes."

Brantville picked up the stack of paper. "I determined to write one of my own, an autobiography," he said to Holt, "and in your partner I saw an amanuensis and editor of wit and craft." He gestured with what Holt now realized was a manuscript. "Here is the product of our labors, holed up here while you tended the animals." Brantville turned to Sam. "You have talent—the talent of a professional."

He put down the manuscript and went to the shelves,

prised out a copy of *Harper's Illustrated Weekly* magazine. A slip marked the page he sought, which he displayed so both of them could see it. An article about the timber industry in northern Idaho was bylined "Samantha Lowell," and beside it was a line drawing of the author.

"You appear different, yet not that different," Brantville said.

Sam looked at Holt, whose turn it was now to shake his head. They had changed their looks somewhat. Holt's hair, razor-cut to a stubble in prison as a precaution against ubiquitous lice, hung over his collar by now, and at Sam's suggestion he'd grown a mustache, though he drew the line at a beard. "I'd look like a hooligan and feel like a fool," he'd complained. Sam, for her part, had cropped off most of her ash-blond tresses and dyed what was left an auburn color. It made her look boyish, though Holt thought it suited her.

But Sam's train of thought was on a different track. She nodded to Brantville, said, "It's me. I'm sorry we deceived you."

Brantville seemed to take acceptance of the apology under advisement. "A man and a woman ride into my spread and request employment," he explained, thinking aloud. "The woman triggers something familiar in my memory, which remains keen despite my years. The woman is well-lettered, while the man evinces a nature that suggests deliberation and some experience with the less savory aspects of violent encounters." Brantville drank. "This is not customary."

He indicated the drawing in the magazine. "When I put you together with the woman in this magazine, I wondered why you would give up your career."

"Romance?" Sam suggested discreetly. For the past two months, Holt had slept in the bunkhouse, while she occupied a room upstairs.

"But I saw it wasn't so. You are close, but not in that way. What could link you, I wondered."

Again Brantville hesitated. "The winters are long and dark on these northern plains, and lonely. I have Eliza—

Mrs. Maplethorn—but between us, she can be more trouble than she is worth. And I like a good tale, something to chew on during the cold season."

Brantville got up to reshelf the magazine, then bent to feed two chunks of cordwood to the fire. Sparks rose up the flue.

Sam gazed at Holt. "Tell him."

"Why?" Holt demanded.

"Because he wishes to help."

"Is that true?" Holt asked Brantville.

Brantville regarded him. "Yes," he said finally, "if I feel morally able after hearing your story."

Time passed, and then Holt sighed. "I believe I'll have that drink after all," he said.

Brantville listened patiently and without interruption, though Holt felt himself rambling at the start. He worked to order it chronologically, and by and by the narrative took form.

He began with his career as an itinerant lawman, and the ways in which it brought him to a silver-mining camp called Argentville in the high mountains of Colorado and smack-dab into the middle of a power struggle between a capitalist named Fitzsimmons and a criminal boss named Jack Stringer. His mistake, Holt told Brantville there in the study, was to take his job as town marshal seriously; he believed that a peace officer's mandate was to maintain the peace.

Both Fitzsimmons and Stringer, though rivals, thought otherwise. When Holt's efforts became a threat to the financial well-being of both, one of them—Holt could not say which—saw to it that he was framed for murder.

The victim was a madam named Cat Lacey, and despite her profession, she and Holt developed a relationship that at least bordered on love. On the most grievous morning of his life, after a night of blackout-hard drinking, Holt awakened with his hand on the hilt of a knife that was fatally buried in Cat's breast.

Fitzsimmons and Stringer were both men of power, and Holt had one edge only: an eyewitness, one of Cat's girls, who saw a misformed giant of a man leave Cat's room via the window. But it carried no weight. Holt was arrested, charged with the crime, provided with a crooked lawyer in the employ of Fitzsimmons or Stringer, convicted, and sentenced to life without parole in the federal penitentiary at Yuma, Arizona. There he languished for a year and a half.

In the study, Brantville studied Sam. "And here is where you enter the story," he guessed.

"To my lasting regret," Sam said, solemn and teasing.

Holt grinned. "I appreciate that." To Brantville, Holt said, "We sort of got stuck with each other."

All his days, Holt had seen his life as a ledger of luck, bad fortune on the recto, good on the verso. The former listed the frame-up, along with the minié ball that almost ended his natural life, the death of Cat Lacey, and his current status as a piece of meat worth five thousand dead or alive to anyone wishing to put another bullet in his back. The latter pretty much added up to Sam, and her trust and loyalty in siding him.

Before she'd taken her chance on him, she was the first female correspondent for *Harper's* ever assigned to the frontier. In this capacity, she'd set out to write an article on the Yuma prison. There she'd met Holt, and when he told his story to her, she had for some thank-the-heavens reason come not only to believe him, but to understand that the giant man, the true perpetrator, was the key to his exoneration.

Without regard to her own future, she'd arranged to bust him out.

Late at night on the trail, lying sleepless in his bedroll listening to Sam's regular breathing, Holt found himself in the next months occasionally struck with melancholy at his responsibility for the sacrifice she had made. Her people, back in Boston, were of respectable stock, no doubt wounded by the fact that their daughter was an outlaw with a price on her head, somewhere absorbed into the vastness of the West but subject at any given moment to arrest and the unimaginable dismalness of a life behind bars. But the choice was hers, not his; for better or worse, he was—

"Stuck with me?" Sam echoed Holt's comment, as Brantville watched, almost amused. "Is that how you see it?"

"I was kidding," Holt said.

Brantville was in thrall to their history by this point. "What then?" he demanded, every bit like a child caught up in a bedtime story.

Within a month of Holt's break from the Yuma prison, when the present gray-bearded summer was still in the flower of youth, the path he and Sam followed led to a Utah town called Golem. In the course of helping its citizens resist a jack Mormon named Lemuel Baynes, Holt learned more about the man who had committed the murder for which he was condemned.

His name was Gutt, and the Golemites feared him as a monster. In nature's way, he was. Gutt suffered from a birth defect called gigantism, a cruel, freakish trick that enlarged his frame in grotesque fashion. He stood nearly seven feet tall, and the bones of his face were exaggerated so greatly, he looked like some creature from a picture book about prehistoric times.

Holt knew this firsthand, because there had been a confrontation. Holt, through God's luck, came away from it in one piece, and with two items of information.

First, Gutt was almost assuredly the murderer of Cat Lacey. Second, Gutt swore to kill Holt as well if Holt continued to harry him.

Frightened as he was, Holt had no choice but to pursue, with Sam insistently siding him. Gutt's confession—and Holt had no idea how it could be compelled from him—was the single key to lifting the labels of fugitive and killer from Holt's head.

* * *

Gutt was long gone and summer had barely arrived when they successfully ramrodded the cattle drive that meant the victory of Golem over the Mormon Elder Baynes. The rest of the season saw them riding north, following Gutt's scent.

In the isolated towns of the far-spread West, talk was a principal recreation, and the big man's coarse, distorted features caused comment wherever he passed. The trail led them past Salt Lake City and on to Wyoming, up Wind River, across Jackson Hole and into the Yellowstone country, lately designated a National Park, whatever that was. Always Gutt had passed through a day or two or three before, his track warm but never hot. They followed the Yellowstone River out of the park, and that put them in Montana Territory.

At the village of Lewistown the track petered out.

In a local watering hole they met a man named Jergensen. He sported a freshly broken leg and was in the process of taking on whiskey by way of anesthetic against the pain. Jergensen shared his circumstances: A couple days previously, he'd been thrown when his horse was startled by a grizzly bear. Jergensen, as Holt and Sam drank with him, was entering the morose segment of his determined drunk. He felt badly not only for himself, but for leaving his boss one hand short in the middle of the season.

Holt and Sam were nursing short beers, because the ten cents each they cost left no more than pocket change between them. What sort of a place was this spread where he had worked, Holt inquired of Jergensen, and what sort of man was his boss? Jergensen painted a picture that Holt had been a part of much of his early years, of a spread where men worked hard and minded their own business.

It was worth the chance, they decided, that they'd be accepted at face value. If so, it meant respite from what had become an increasingly draining life flavored by the continual low-level tension that the next stranger they met would recognize them. Equally important, it meant money in their jeans.

"That was the chance we took." Holt stood once more at

the window of the rancher's office, staring into the gathering darkness.

Brantville came up beside him. "Do you give me your word, man to man, that what you have told me is the truth?"

"It is," Holt said.

Brantville considered for a full minute. "So be it." He produced a Hamilton watch from his vest pocket, consulted it. "I'll turn in," he said. "We'll ponder further in the morning."

"What's to ponder?" Holt stood.

"Your future," Brantville pronounced.

"Just so it doesn't include any more bucking broncos."

Brantville drained the last of his drink. "Saddle your own horse," he said, "and be ready to ride in the morning." He yawned, nodded politely to Sam, and left them alone.

It was a gesture of trust that Holt found touching. Sam rose, and he felt awkward. "Well then," he said.

She walked him to the door without touching him, and on the porch said good night. By now Holt was behind three whiskeys and just on the borderline of foolishness. Sam may have sensed that, because before he could act, she disappeared back inside.

Half the men had turned in; the rest were engaged in a quiet poker game beneath the glow of an oil lamp, accompanied by the last half-quart of whiskey. Holt played a dozen hands, drank two more drinks, lost ten dollars of their stake, and excused himself to go out back and drain his snake. The night sky was clear and star-spackled, and seemed to offer promise. He went back inside, ignored the temptation to rejoin the game, stripped down to his union suit, and wrapped himself in his sheets.

He fell asleep contemplating vague thoughts of hope, possibility, and of Sam.

Chapter Three

"I'm preoccupied," Holt said.

Sam cantered her horse around so she was facing him. "Why, that explains everything," she said broadly. "I thought you were merely antisocial."

"Huh?"

Sam pulled out her watch. "That's the first words you've said since nine o'clock. If you'd held out a few minutes more, you could have broken the three-hour mark." Sam snapped the watch case shut. "And what is the nature of your preoccupation?"

"This and that," Holt said, and shut up again. That got him a snort of exasperation. What he wished to air was a nagging notion that his destiny was no longer his own, but articulation would not come.

Upon sleeping on the issues, Brantville had come to the conclusion that he would lend them a hand. In fact, guessing that they were hardly flush with dough, and knowing the difficulty of a woman finding ranch work without a recommendation, he'd made telegraphic contact with a fellow member of the Stock Grower's Association on the trip to Lewistown two days earlier to fetch the payroll. Stanley Morgan raised cows near a town called Lobo, fifty miles northwest and across the Missouri, and was willing to take Holt and Sam on.

By now they'd put seven or so of those miles behind them. "I hope this Morgan has permanent work," Holt said.

Sam rolled her eyes; another ten minutes had passed

since their last exchange. "Must your conversation come in fits and starts?"

"I liked not being on the run for a couple months," Holt said. "I wouldn't mind settling down again."

Sam did not reply, and Holt tried to retreat from his thoughts by taking in this country. The previous evening in Brantville's office, he'd been mildly startled to see by the calendar that October had passed and November was upon them. Still, Indian summer clung on tenaciously, the sky a canopy of unbroken blue and the temperature mild enough that Holt was comfortable in shirt and leather vest. The sun was low but bright on the rolling plains covered in brown grass, broken here and there by a steep-skirted butte. Off to the right cottonwoods marked the course of the Missouri, and a little ways back they'd cut a wagon road that Brantville told them led to a ferry, a dozen miles or so upriver from a landing town called Fort Benton.

Holt's stomach rumbled and he was about to suggest a lunch break when Sam pointed. "Thar she blows," she announced in an exaggerated tone.

They followed the road through a cut that led down to the river shore, where a woven cable ran across the water, anchored in buried cement blocks and looped matching tripods of cross-bucked wooden ties. A ferryman emerged from the soddy and demanded six bits in advance.

"Why six bits?" Holt asked.

"Twenty-five cents each for you and the horses." The ferryman was an odd-looking duck, thin from the waist down, but with heavily muscled arms and shoulders developed in the course of his work. "Ladies ride free. Rule of the house."

He pullied them across the shallow sluggish river on a flat-bottomed barge hooked to the cable, and left them on the far bank without so much as an adios. Maybe they'd interrupted his dinner. "Let's water the horses and eat," Holt suggested.

Miz Maplethorn had made them a gift of provisions for the trip, including several sandwiches, slices of the previous night's roast beef between thick slabs of wheat bread. They ate seated against tree trunks, basking in the midday sun.

Holt figured Sam was irked at him for clamming up, but when she spoke, her tone was thoughtful, even wary. "Settling down would be fine, if it were an option," she said. "But I don't think Gutt is going to come to us."

"Time changes situations, and it's on our side. The longer we stay free—and holding up on some back-country ranch is a good move in that direction—the sooner people will forget."

"Not Pert."

Clennon Pert was the U.S. Federal Marshal who was pursuing them, and with whom they'd already had one run-in in Utah.

"He's got to find us first."

"We've got to find Gutt," Sam insisted.

Holt looked at her, and she turned from his gaze. "I was about to tell you a secret," he said. "Now I'm wondering if you've got one of your own."

A magpie alit on the grass a few feet from them. Sam tossed her bread crust, and the cheeky scavenger hardly flinched, but grabbed the morsel up in its beak and hopped back to enjoy it.

"Early on, when we arrived at Brantville's ranch, I told him we were seeking Gutt," Sam admitted.

Holt kept his temper. "You don't think that was risky?"

"Not very. I knew he had friends around the territory, and I made up some lie about why we wished to find him. Brantville was polite enough to pretend to believe me, and discreet enough to know that my confiding in him might not set well with you."

Before they left that morning, Brantville had taken Sam aside. Holt assumed it was a private moment of thanks for her help with his memoirs.

"During the time we were working for him," Sam said, "Brantville did ask about Gutt whenever he had occasion to wire his colleagues. He came up empty—until he contacted

WINTER OF THE WOLF

this Morgan. Gutt, or someone looking a lot like him, has been seen in Lobo within the past week."

The magpie moved closer, like a house pet begging for table scraps. "I thought you might get cold feet," Sam added. "You've still got the opportunity."

Holt put aside the implied challenge for the moment. "What's he doing in this Lobo town?"

"Wolfing."

"That tells me little."

Sam plucked Holt's pouch from his pocket and went to work on post-luncheon cigarettes. "A couple years back, Brantville and his fellow ranchers successfully lobbied the Territorial Legislature to place a bounty on wolves, from a belief that they preyed on livestock, which may or may not be true. A rough class of men took up the offer. Gutt is apparently among them."

Holt took the cigarette she offered, lit up and fumigated his brain. "You are convinced that we must run him to earth and make him talk."

"I am."

Holt climbed to his feet, went down to the water's edge and took up the bridle straps of the two horses. Here it was again, he thought, that being led around as if he were on a rein himself. "Then we'd best be moving on," he said.

They spotted Fort Benton from a high cut-bank bluff as the sun touched the mountains off to the west. About a mile distant, residences spread back from a main street with commercial buildings running along the waterfront and facing several piers. A steamboat was docked at one. It looked to be a substantial enough village to have regular law enforcement, and besides, Holt was loath to spend any of their hard-earned stake on hotel rooms when the night proposed to be no colder than a light frost.

They camped by a nameless tributary with plenty of dry driftwood for a fire. Holt made coffee and cooked salt pork in a pot of tinned beans, courtesy of Miz Maplethorn, and for dessert there were apples from her root cellar. With the last of the coffee, they smoked and studied the stars, and Holt's mind was serene, enough so that when Sam murmured, "You never told me your secret," he momentarily forgot the earlier conversation.

"I'm feeling guilty," he blurted.

"And all the while I believed you were innocent," she teased.

He squinted at her. "About you." Holt sat up straighter, his back against a log. "You had a life before you crossed my trail," he said, fumbling with his notions. "You had . . ."

"A career?" she finished.

"Something to look forward to." Their horses, picketed within reach of the stream, looked over at the sound of voices. "What you got now," Holt went on, "is no money and no future beyond a life in jail, we make one wrong move."

Slowly she shook her head. "I'll never see the inside of a prison cell." She laughed. "Unless I'm visiting you."

"That's rich," Holt said darkly.

Sam finished her coffee. "Holt," she said more seriously, "allow me to tell you how the cow eats the cabbage. There is such a thing as the ruling class. My father is among its members. He knows senators; twice he has dined with the President."

Her point soaked in slowly, its ramifications elusive. "You mean that Gutt doesn't matter?" he tried. "Your father could get this all fixed?"

"Of course."

"Then why are you with me?"

She rose, stared down at him. "Are you a complete idiot?" She went off into the brush without waiting for an answer. Holt checked on the horses, did his own business, went back to lay out the bedrolls. Sam returned.

"Yes," Holt said.

"Yes what?"

"Yes I'm an idiot, and why are you here if you don't have to be?"

"Because I want to, you idiot."

To Holt's vast ill-ease, Sam's tone was unmistakably tender.

For a long sleepless time after they turned in, Holt listened to Sam's breathing and grappled with emotions. In his mind they appeared as a menu from which he could make any number of choices. He settled on bewilderment, taking it down into the darkness with him as he drifted off to sleep.

Chapter Four

"There is a certain odor attendant to this place," Holt said, keeping his voice low and leaning in the saddle toward Sam.

"I thought I smelled something," she said.

Holt had visited some rude mining camps in his travels, but those were tent cities; he'd never seen a permanent settlement as coarse as this town of Lobo. The fact that the half-dozen or so buildings were made of wood was more likely due to the abundant stands of Doug fir and ponderosa pine on the slopes of the craggy, already-snowcapped peaks a mile or so to the west than to pride of residence, as they were rudely built of rough-planed planks and completely unadorned. Along the rutted path that served for Lobo's main and only street, they consisted of a few cabins, livery barn, mercantile, and saloon. The last was the only two-story structure, the upper floor likely living quarters for the tavern keeper. A few horses were tethered at a hitching post in front, and before them a badly hand-painted sign identified the establishment as "Quint's."

"There is the place to make inquiry, if we must," Holt said. "I got a hunch we should steer clear, find Morgan's spread on our own."

"We could end up wandering the prairie for who knows how long," Sam countered.

Holt hated it when she was right. "I'll see what I can find out," he conceded. "You—"

"Wait here," Sam finished for him. "No." She smiled. "What if I'm accosted? I'd be defenseless."

She was needling him. Early in their time together, Holt had taught her the use of the Colt's .38 revolver she wore holstered on her hip, and she'd since been blooded, compelled to shoot a man in the leg to save Holt's life.

"All right," he conceded. "Only let's just do our business and get out of here. This town gives me the willies."

Holt gazed east, toward where Morgan's spread lay. As was often the topological case along the flank of the northern Rockies, the terrain turned abruptly flat, becoming rangeland that was neither the best nor worst Holt had seen in his days. Abundant bunch grass dotted the scrub, and with the rights to enough land, it was viable cow-growing territory—and one hell of a lot more attractive than this Lobo town.

"Let's hope no one steals the horses," Holt said as Sam climbed down.

"From the looks of this place," she said, "I bet it's an everyday occurrence."

Deformities were hardly uncommon among the citizens eking out existence along the frontier. Miners who packed too much giant powder into a drill hole gripped shot glasses with the two fingers they had left; ex-cowhands wore shirts pinned up to the shoulder above phantom arms lost to gangrene after roping accidents; timberjacks staggered like drunken sailors on stumps of legs from which they had inadvertently chopped their own feet.

"Go ahead and stare," the man behind the bar said. "I'm used to it."

The part of the anatomy the barkeep was missing, though, was a new one on Holt. Improbably and horrifically, the left side of his jaw was gone. In its stead, from below his nose to the curve of his chin, was a steel plate.

"What'll you have?" the barkeep asked.

Holt recalled a story he'd considered apocryphal, told by a prospector in the Sangre de Cristo Mountains of Colorado. Attached to the tale was the name on the sign out front. "You'd be Mr. Quint."

"You've heard of me," Quint said, in a voice as mechanical as his facial prosthesis.

"Bourbon would be fine," Sam said.

This did not strike Holt as the best time for a leisurely libation. He'd regretted entering this watering hole the moment they walked through the bat-wing doors. He could see at least half a dozen reasons it was a bad idea, premier among them the men scattered among the tables wearing buffalo robes despite the mildness of the day, as if it were some sort of uniform. He added in the lack of amenity, which was limited to a low ceiling, this plank and sawbuck counter that served as a bar, and the lurid leer with which every eye regarded Sam.

Quint's steel jaw was icing on the cake. The barkeep set out glasses, poured, and said, "Two bucks."

Holt knew he was being jerked around, but prudence told him not to make an issue of it. He placed a brace of silver dollars on the bar. Quint made a pass and they disappeared into his big mitt. Everything about the man was oversized: his hands, girth, and personality. He towered a good half foot over Holt.

"Can you direct us to the ranch of Stanley Morgan?" Sam asked.

Quint studied her, as did every other pair of eyes in this place. Although he had not remarked on it, Holt did note as they rode in under the midday sun that Lobo was lacking a whorehouse. From the gazes Sam was drawing, Holt warranted such an establishment would do profitable business.

"What would you want with Stanley Morgan?" Quint said.

Holt didn't know what answer would best benefit him, and while he was considering, the conversation veered south.

"Ask me," Quint said, obviously referring to his steel jaw.

Holt's discomfiture waxed. The wolfers evinced an air of anticipation, as if this were a drama they'd seen before, but such a favorite as to merit repeat viewing.

"You can tell when they want it," Quint said. "She wanted it."

Quint turned to the back bar, a simple plank shelf, and poured a generous splash of amber whiskey into a glass. "I took her, turned on her stomach like a barnyard animal, gave her what she asked for. She had eyes like a doe."

Holt sensed serious mania here, and something else as well: a bullying attitude that might disguise pusillanimity. He touched at Sam's elbow, and to his distress she said to Quint, "Who wanted it?" She had taken on her reporter's mien, the need to hear any story no matter what abomination it promised.

"I was doing her like that when the buck came in." Quint drank his whiskey. "No wonder I hate Indians. The son of a bitch shot me in the face."

Quint looked down into his glass, as if the darkness of the whiskey dregs mirrored his soul. "My mates laid me out on the bed of a buckboard. The pain was horrific. I lived on bile and booze for a day and a night and then we were in Great Falls. There I was made whole." He tapped the nail of his forefinger on the steel plate; the sound it made set Holt's skin to crawling.

"I survived," Quint said, "and came around with a hatred of women, red and white and any other color of the spectrum."

Sam's expression remained neutral. Holt cleared his throat and said, "I guess we'll be moseying."

Quint stretched his arm across the bar and let his hand hover just above the vee of Sam's blouse. "I ain't had a woman in two days, nor fought a man in a week," Quint said. "What'll it be?"

The silence of the bar was broken by a rapping below the rim of the countertop. The sound climbed up, and Sam showed Quint the gun in her hand.

Quint frowned. "The fight, then," he said, but reluctantly, as if this were not going as he planned.

Holt saw what was about to happen, and was ready as Quint lunged over the bar at him. Holt drove his fist hard into Quint's extended gut and scuttled to one side. Quint went down hard on the filthy plank floor, and to Holt's surprise, he wore a look of apprehension when he rolled over.

The bullying manner was an act after all, Holt decided, and Quint had no true belly for a fight. Quint fought to recover enough breath to ask, "What is your business with Morgan?"

"No business," Sam said, her gun aimed at Quint. "He has offered a job of work."

Quint got to his knees, averting his eyes from Holt, and it appeared he was ready to back off.

Someone laughed.

Quint's expression went dark as midnight. He gathered his feet and launched himself into Holt.

Holt swung and missed. Quint used Holt's momentum to spin him around, got his arms laced through Holt's elbows. Quint frog-marched him across the room and rammed his body through the bat-wing doors, released him so he tumbled into the street by the horses. Holt scrambled to his feet and found himself face-to-face with the man.

Quint punched him in the stomach, but Holt managed to twist to one side and the blow was glancing. Holt swung at Quint's chin, stopped himself a fraction of an inch from breaking his hand on Quint's steel plate. Quint took advantage to catch him squarely in the gut.

Holt went down again and Quint was atop him.

"So it's Morgan you seek. If you insist." Quint punched him in the face, then backed off.

Blood pooled in Holt's eye socket. Through its red veil he saw men streaming from the saloon to watch. He swung wildly and hit nothing but air.

"Follow the wagon trace through town," Quint said. "Turn east, and three miles on you'll see Morgan's spread." Quint slammed his massive fist into the point of Holt's chin.

Holt sat down hard in the rutted street. Almost solicitously, Quint said. "You got all that?"

"Yeah," Holt said. "Thanks." He wanted to pass out, but that didn't seem about to happen.

"Good," Quint said. "Now ride out in the other direction or face more of my wrath."

"Maybe," Holt muttered.

Quint advanced and readied himself to kick in Holt's ribs.

Holt rolled away, heard a sharp cracking sound, and Quint crashed facedown beside him, lay still. Sam stood with her legs slightly apart and her gun clubbed in her hand.

Holt climbed shakily to his feet, wiped blood from his face with his neckerchief. The feel of the cartilage grating in his nose made him nauseous. He wanted to boot Quint as the vicious sadist had meant to do him, but he forestalled. The last few minutes had seen enough mindless violence.

"He broke my beak," Holt said.

"It doesn't look so bad," Sam said. The wolfers remained before the saloon, watching as this show went on. "Go away," Sam said. To Holt's mild surprise, they filed back inside.

Sam touched him with a steadying hand. "You okay to ride?"

"As long as it's out of here." Holt followed her to the horses. "And the next time I get a hunch to steer clear of someplace," he went on peevishly, "let's by God steer clear."

Chapter Five

Holt's nose had ceased to drool blood, but it and most of the rest of his face still hurt a half hour later when they reached the first clump of what were likely Morgan's cows. They grazed at the bank of a stream that must have a bed of limestone, because its water was the color of runny milk. They reined up halfway across and let their horses drink.

"It's too bad we had to give Fort Benton a pass," Sam said casually. They'd skirted the river port after breakfasting, four hours, ten miles, and one beating previous. "It's a pretty little town. I was there two years ago."

"You are trying to jolly me up," Holt observed. "I don't want to be jollied."

He'd descended into a funk in the half hour since they'd ridden out of Lobo, comprised of equal parts of pain and shame, of his broken nose and of having lost a fight in front of Sam. "What the hell was that all about anyway?" Holt said.

"It did seem a little off base," Sam agreed. "I got the feeling that Quint didn't expect you to fight back, and went a little nuts when you did. Something about him says that his bullying masks a touch of the yellow streak."

"One sure thing is he's no pal of Morgan," Holt said, "nor did he appreciate that we might be." He looked over at her. "So why didn't he just gun us down? Those men didn't look the type to raise objection."

"Cold-blooded murder is always tricky business," Sam said, as if they were debating tomorrow's weather. "He probably figured you were cowed enough to turn tail and leave his territory."

"I'm wondering why we haven't," Holt muttered.

But they both knew the answer—the possible presence of Gutt, for one, and thank the Lord he hadn't been in the saloon. And the other issue, which they understood without having discussed it, a lesson learned in their escapade in Utah: living a life on the run, they could not afford to show the white feather too often, lest retreat become a disabling habit.

"I wrote a story that touched on Fort Benton," Sam said, refusing to embrace his mood. "Would you like to hear it?"

Before them was a sea of grass, turning brown and curing up with the change of season, but still nourishing to livestock. "Love to," Holt said pettishly.

"Why thank you, Mr. Holt," Sam said tartly. "I appreciate the favor of your audience."

The riverside town's existence went back to 1821, Sam told Holt as they rode past increasing numbers of free-ranging cows, and its situation marked the head of the navigable waters of the Missouri. Indeed, she guessed, it was probably from Benton that the wolfers shipped their pelts east.

But it was not so much the town that she had come to limn in an article for her magazine, but its role in the fate of one of the more illustrious and mysterious players in Montana's early history, a larger-than-life character named Thomas Francis Meagher.

"Meagher was an Irishman from Waterford," Sam said, "a rogue and adventurer who packed more escapades into his years than any ten average men. His career began as a ringleader of the Irish independence movement that followed the potato famine. It appeared to be over when he was arrested for sedition in 1848 and sentenced to be hanged, drawn, and quartered."

"Kill him then torture him," Holt muttered. "I love the

way the law thinks." But the story at least was taking his mind from its dark thoughts.

"Queen Victoria commuted the sentence to exile on Van Dieman's Land," Sam continued. "It's an island—"

"South of Australia," Holt interrupted.

"Aren't we the know-it-all," Sam teased. "Guess what happened next."

"I haven't the faintest idea."

"Then be quiet and listen," Sam admonished. "In 1852 he escaped—no one knows how—and went to Brazil. Next he popped up in New York, where he established a newspaper called the *Irish News*, took American citizenship, and became a lecturer known throughout the East. In his spare time he explored Central America. About that time, the Civil War broke out."

"This was probably a boon from his point of view," Holt opined. "Give him something new to do."

"Exactly," Sam confirmed. "He formed the Sixty-ninth New York Regiment, which came to be known as the 'Bloody Irish' and the scourge of the Confederacy. When the war ended, Meagher was a brigadier general."

"Good for him."

"Exceedingly," Sam said dryly. "With the North having prevailed, he'd made a lot of powerful friends, not the least among them President Johnson. It's a fair bet that at this point he'd never heard of Montana; next thing he knew, he was appointed secretary of the territory. That's the equivalent of governor if this was a state."

Holt was drawn into the story despite himself. "This Meagher sounds like some job of work."

"He was that and more, a brilliant orator and a pathological drunkard who ruled like a dictator. I talked to a dozen people who knew him well, and to a man, they either revered or reviled him. That's what makes the ending of the story so intriguing."

"Here is where Fort Benton comes in," Holt guessed.

"There, Meagher boarded a steamer on the first day of July in 1867," she confirmed. "He'd made a lot of friends and even more enemies, political and personal. That night a sentry on the boat saw a figure dressed in white moving around the stern, and then heard a splash. Meagher disappeared, and no body was ever found, nor was anyone implicated in foul play, despite allegations involving everyone from the Republicans to the vigilantes, and the offer of a ten thousand dollar reward for his killer."

Having had its fill, Holt's bay gelding raised its head and looked about, perhaps sensing from the livestock that they were nearing their destination.

"He was forty-four years old," Sam said.

"That's a lot of living to pack into such a span." Holt, still feeling morose in the aftermath of the fight in Lobo, contemplated the times when he considered those in their forties to be his elders. Now that he was only a half-dozen years south of the mark himself, his perspective was changed. "How old are you?" he asked.

"Wouldn't you like to know." Sam laughed, once again acting like she was inside his head. Truth to tell, he had been wondering....

"Time to ride on in and make our introductions." Sam jerked on the reins of her roan and walked it the rest of the way across the creek.

Holt followed, scowling. Here he was, partnered with this woman in increasingly intricate ways, and he didn't even know her age.

Like the Brantville ranch, Morgan's was trim and spruce, the utter opposite of the nearby town where Holt had his recent misadventure. The buildings, however, were given more to utility than finery.

The big house, as a rancher's headquarters was invariably known, was not really that big, a one-story cabin of chinked logs with a single window aside the hinged plank door. It stood upwind from an extensive feedlot and corral system comprising at least a dozen pens. To one side was a whitewashed barn, to the other several haystacks, one exposed, the others covered with canvas tarp. A ditch cut in from the creek filled a stock tank and watered a kitchen garden gone to weed this late in the season. The remainder of the outpost comprised a bunkhouse, a well pump, a chicken coop, and a privy off away from the water supply.

As they reined up before the cabin, someone behind them said, "Reach for the sky."

Holt had a healthy distaste for guns on his back, and did as he was told. Sam, however, raised one hand and eased her horse around with the other. When nothing untoward occured, Holt did the same.

Before the bunkhouse, a woman held a Winchester lever-action aimed in their direction. Somewhere in her twenties, she wore a long gray duster and a Stetson over a mess of cascading blond hair that framed high cheekbones, a well-formed visage, and eyes that shined with a hint of craziness. "State your business," the woman demanded.

This was Holt's day for voices behind his back. A new one said, "Stop this nonsense."

The woman grumbled inaudibly, lowered the rifle, and dug at the barnyard dirt with her boot toe like a petulant child. A man passed their horses, went to her and took the weapon. "She reads them books and gets notions," he said, which made no particular sense to Holt.

"You'd be Mr. Morgan," he ventured, although the man did not fit Holt's preconception. He was dressed slovenly in coveralls and a cloth jacket over a red union suit. Beneath a straw hat, a cigarette dangled from lips surrounded by a weathered face, and Holt thought there was a bit of a drunken roll to his gait.

"I'm Prospect," the man said. "It's my brother you seek. Climb down and we'll search him out." He waved the woman over. "See to their horses."

She did as ordered, but not before giving Holt a frank up and down look. "Charity," she said.

"This way." Prospect turned for the cabin, trailing a whiff of liquor smell.

As they followed, Holt ducked his head toward Sam and said in a low voice, "Is everyone but me talking in code?"

Sam smiled as Prospect pushed open the door. "Don't worry," she said. "We'll crack it soon enough."

" 'Ye shall return every man unto his family,' " Stanley Morgan said.

"Leviticus 25:10," Holt cited.

Morgan looked impressed. "You are a religious man?"

"I'm a man whose primer was the Good Book. My folks moved us around quite a bit, and there wasn't carrying room for much of a library."

"Homesteaders? Then you've had some ranching experience."

"Enough to tell one end of a cow from the other," Holt said.

"Our father was home-tutored as well, and developed a fondness for romance. Thus such names as Prospect and Charity." He smiled wanly. "My brother fell on hard times, and I took him in."

Prospect scowled and gravitated toward a shelf below the front window, where a corked bottle of dark liquor was flanked by water tumblers. The interior of Morgan's cabin was surprisingly capacious. This living room occupied the front two-thirds, and in the back was a bedroom and kitchen side by side. Some attention had been given to homeliness: Line drawings from magazines were tacked to the log walls, a neatly surfaced rolltop desk faced the corner where the light was best, and a handmade dining table with six chairs, wooden and straight-backed but cushioned with quilted pillows, sat near to a fat-bellied wood stove.

"Miss Charity," Sam said delicately. "Is she . . . ?"

"Dotty?" Morgan said. " 'Willful' might be the better adjective, as 'feckless' applies to her father, my brother."

Prospect poured himself a drink, the gesture defiant, but Holt was not so interested in Morgan's familial affairs. "Mr. Brantville said you had work for us."

A pot sat on the stove, and from it Morgan poured coffee. He set cups on the table. "That is what this interview is about, Mr. Holt."

Holt kept his expression neutral. It appeared that Teddy Brantville had sent another wire while he and Sam were on the trail. Holt didn't much like that.

Morgan sat down. "I do need hands," he said, "but I require other skills as well. I face a threat."

"Quint," Holt guessed.

"You've met him," Morgan said, not asking. "I suppose it was he who mashed your nose."

Holt saved away the comment. "What skills exactly are you seeking in your ranch hands?"

Morgan took some of his coffee. "Some experience with violent ways," he said.

Holt set his palms on the table. "I have done some chores," he said, "but I've never worked as a hired gun."

"Hear me out," Morgan said mildly. "My friend Teddy told me this: you and Miss Lowell wish to find a man who may be among the wolfers. I will give you a base from which to smoke him out, and I will pay you well."

Sam, who had been observing all this in studied silence, spoke for the first time. "How well?"

"Fifty dollars each per month, for as long as the job takes."

"That's a superior price," Sam said, "but still you've not explained what you believe it will purchase."

Morgan went to the window. "When I came to this country, it was a garden," he said. "That was after the war, and almost simultaneous with the arrival of Quint."

The door opened and Charity entered. She took the now-empty coffeepot into the kitchen, while her father re-addressed the liquor bottle. Morgan frowned absently at Prospect's back.

"A minor gold rush brought Quint here, and in its course he established himself," he said. "He managed to pan several thousand dollars' worth, which he invested in building his saloon and mercantile. From the beginning, he was associated with shady doings—hijacking helpless pilgrims, crooked gambling, some desultory rustling—though no

WINTER OF THE WOLF

charge was ever made to stick. We had no law, and have none still."

"You and Quint were in conflict from the start," Sam guessed.

"Quint is blessed with luck," Morgan said. "Most camps go bust when a gold strike runs out, but before that could happen, Lobo became a way station for drovers trailing cattle to summer range in Canada and back again in the autumn. By and by this business petered out as homesteaders came in and fenced the range, yet once again fortune smiled on Quint when we stock growers got the wolfing law passed. Those who came to take profit from it rely on Quint for gear, provisions, and liquor."

"You mentioned homesteaders, but you pretty much seem to have this territory to yourself."

"I bought them out and gave them a fair price," Morgan said. "It was a boon; otherwise they would have gone belly up and abandoned their property for no remuneration. This is decent country, but not such in which you can make an agricultural living on a mere three hundred twenty acres." Morgan stood, went to the window. "I prospered, but now I am beset."

"By Quint?" Holt asked.

"From all sides." Morgan turned to face them. Charity gave him an odd look, as if she knew what was coming next. "Quint and the Blackfeet," Morgan said.

Sam looked confused. "Indians," Holt explained, though he wasn't following this much better than she.

"I've coexisted peacefully with the natives," Morgan said. "Occasionally they help themselves to one of my beeves, but never more than three animals a year and only when game is scarce. In exchange, they make me presents of clothing and trade goods that by their lights are of equal value. Never mind; I consider the cows they appropriate to be fair recompense for what we have taken from them."

Charity returned to set the coffeepot on the stove, darted a flirtatious glance at Holt.

"But this season," Morgan continued, "I have lost over a dozen animals."

"Not to the Blackfeet," Charity said.

"Hush up," Morgan said. "I've got as good as a confession. I am on speaking terms with the chief. He admitted that some of his braves are beyond his control, but denied either involvement or gain."

"Did you believe him?" Sam asked.

"I don't know. Quint definitely wishes to drive me out, and the Indians have a motive as well."

"Start with Quint." To Holt's mind he was the more formidable threat, especially with that band of ruffians at his apparent disposal. "What's he got against you?"

"I represent the civilization that is bound to come to these parts and is antithetical to Quint's ambitions. There is talk that the Northern Pacific will lay track through here, which will make small ranching and farming far more feasible, and will bring in a flood of decent people who will look dimly on such as Quint."

Morgan extended a second finger. "In the meantime, Quint can make a small fortune simply through thievery of my estate and stock. That is reason enough in itself."

Morgan added a finger to make the final tally. "Lastly comes pure meanness. Quint loathes the Blackfeet, and would be pleasured immensely if he incited a panic that led to a war against them."

Morgan cleared his throat. "You'll excuse us."

Prospect scowled at his brother, but he took the whiskey bottle in one hand and the wrist of his reluctant daughter in the other, marched her out.

Morgan waited until the door closed again. "Teddy Brantville is my friend and colleague," he said. "You will have surmised that he has told me all."

"All of what?"

"Brantville explained your predicament as well as his belief in your innocence," Morgan continued when they were gone. "Quint is likely to take a more venal view, if he knows the facts of the reward."

"That sounds a wee bit like a threat," Sam observed. "My partner doesn't take kindly to threats."

"I'm sorry," Morgan said. "You are my last hope."

"You been running this place by yourself up to now?"

Morgan shook his head. "I had a couple of cowhands until last week. They disappeared along with their gear, so I expect—hope, anyway—that they were run off rather than killed."

"That's cheering," Holt said.

"Run off by the man you seek," Morgan continued. "I saw him lurking around one day." Morgan described him; it was Gutt, all right.

"But the first order of business is to bring my cows in. As you saw when you rode in, I put up irrigated hay and keep the animals on feed through the winter."

"That we can do," Holt said.

"In the course of the roundup, you may have opportunity to find out who is rustling, and to stop it."

"How?"

"With evidence, I can summon the law. I'm not asking you to engage in vigilantism. And when you have completed that, you may find this Gutt."

"That still leaves Quint waiting to pounce, if your estimation of him is on the money."

Morgan looked sheepish, and Holt guessed the omission was deliberate. "One problem at a time," the rancher mumbled.

Holt stood. "We'll have to talk this over," he said finally.

"You do that," Morgan said. "You'll find your belongings in the bunkhouse."

Another item in a checklist of what Holt did not like about this business, but Holt saw no profit in making an issue of it. He cocked his head at Sam, and they got out of there. The cabin, like his situation, was beginning to feel increasingly confining.

Chapter Six

The mountain men who were the first non-native settlers on the high plains of Montana claimed there were only two seasons, and as Holt and Sam slept through their first night on Morgan's ranch, winter dismissed summer with the grim finality of a bouncer ejecting an obstreperous drunk. They arose to four inches of snow in the barnyard, a skim of ice atop the stock tank, slate skies, and an assertive chill in the air.

That the sea change in the weather held off until their arrival was good fortune for Morgan. Many ranchers free-ranged their cattle through the winter, and nine years out of ten the animals managed to survive if not fatten. But one especially vicious season spelled disaster, as had almost happened to Holt's father a few decades earlier. Snow fell by the bucketful and a biting gale drove it into huge drifts in which the poor dumb cows wallowed. Holt and his father managed to bring many of them into the barnyard, where they were tethered and fed on hay loaned by neighbors, but they still lost fully thirty percent of the herd, and at that did better than other ranchers in the area.

He and Sam had debated at some length before accepting Morgan's offer. The telling point was the chance at Gutt. Despite his ambivalent feelings—and fears—about again confronting the big man, Holt must see to his responsibility. Now that Sam had revealed that, unlike him, she was in no constructive danger from the law, he had an obligation to see this business through to a firm resolution, to clear them rather than hope that this predicament would go away like dreams at dawn. If he balked, there was little reason for her to remain with him, and he didn't wish to lose her. This part he did not tell her, although he sensed she suspected his growing attachment....

He did get off his chest some reservations. He disliked Morgan's implied threat if they refused to cooperate, but more significant was a strong hunch that Morgan had not told them everything. Sam had the same sense that they were pawns in Morgan's conflict with Quint. The Lobo boss, if unaware of their true identities, would learn soon enough that he had failed to scare them off. What was unclear was whether Morgan wanted their presence to quell Quint's threats, or to provoke him into some action. The latter seemed logical. If they left while the situation remained unresolved, Morgan was in the same pickle all over again.

Holt's suspicions made for heavy baggage as they rode out for their first day as stock gatherers.

Again to Morgan's luck, the weather grew no harsher, and the roundup went well enough. It took a week, in the saddle dawn to dusk searching out Morgan's three hundred head of summer-fat beeves, automatic, mindless work with a certain serenity to it.

No overt antagonism from Quint nor any Indians interrupted their work. Both Charity and Prospect rode with them, for something to do or to show Morgan they were pulling their load, but on the second day Prospect began nipping from a pint before noon, emptied it within hours, and fell off his horse. Holt laid down the law, and subsequently only Charity joined them.

The girl perplexed Holt. She rode well and could head a recalcitrant cow with grace, but remained an erratic enigma. Sam had opened up to her to the extent of revealing she'd once worked as a writer, and Charity was genuinely interested in Sam's stories. At the same time, Holt could not miss the occasional lascivious looks with which she favored him, although in time he came to be pretty certain it was only flirting. Once in a while, though, Charity's behavior bordered on the lunatic. She might take off across the prairie whooping, or shoot at some varmint for no reason at all. It was as if she was going out of her way to remind them she was not quite right.

On the fourth day, as they were searching the northerly reaches of Morgan's traditional range, Charity disappeared for several hours. When she returned, she was accompanied by an Indian, a tall handsome brave in buckskins. They stopped fifty feet from where Holt was working four cows, and the Blackfeet studied him for a long moment before raising a hand in polite acknowledgment, then making his departure.

When Holt demanded to know what went on, Charity threw one of her silly fits, and he could see he would get nothing from her. He considered mentioning the incident to Morgan, decided to hold it in reserve for the time being. It might profit to have a secret from the rancher.

Holt came to learn that Prospect, while pushing the bounds of whatever accommodation he had with his brother, was careful not to sunder them. Prospect was generally as sullen as his daughter could be manic. In her usual insightful way, Sam opined that this was a form of drunkard's denial: While actually ashamed at his weakness for liquor, Prospect chose to translate it into resentment at his dependence on Morgan's hospitality. The specific details of what had come to form the Morgan ménage had not yet been volunteered.

In any case, Prospect kept himself sober enough to serve as cook, whipping up eggs from the henhouse for their presunrise breakfasts, cold food for their dinners on the prairie, and hearty suppers to fortify their saddle-weary bodies at day's end. They ate with Stanley Morgan in the cabin, with the Pittsburgh stove glowing redly to warm them.

After coffee and cigarettes, Holt and Sam repaired to the bunkhouse, cozy thanks to the fire Holt would build before the evening meal. In a single open room with a ceiling low enough that Holt had to duck his head when moving about, six pallets with thick mattresses lined one wall, with their feet facing the stove. On its other three sides were clothing cupboards and hooks for tack; a sideboard with a water bucket, tin cups, and a washbasin; and a deal table with four chairs and a lantern. A shelf above the sideboard housed playing cards, dominoes, a backgammon set, and several dozen dime novels and back issues of *Harper's*, Sam's magazine. One night she found an article of hers; it was the first Holt had a chance to read all the way through, about a Colorado sharper who fleeced several hundred people with a phony land speculation dodge. She wrote well, he decided, and told her so.

Other nights they played cribbage for a penny a point, or read the fabulous tales of daring desperadoes that Beadle & Adams was so fond of publishing. Holt found it amusing but compelling nonsense that served to take his mind off real life.

They talked little, and Holt knew himself well enough to ken the reason. He was uncomfortable with this forced intimacy, and Sam sensed it. The first night, he tacked a blanket to a rafter to bisect the row of beds, and slept in the one farthest down the line. For her part, Sam took the bunk immediately on the other side, closest to the stove. One time she made some comment about him moving so he could be warmer at night as well, and he'd immediately had a lewd thought about another way he could be warm. He felt a schoolboy's Lutheran guilt, and hoped she wasn't the mind reader he feared her to be.

Winter settled in for a long sojourn. No blue sky penetrated the even-colored cloud cover, and it snowed most days, never heavily but always steadily, so by the end of the week a foot or so had accumulated. Fortunately, the temperature, by the big mercury thermometer nailed up beside the barn door, did not drop below the mid-twenties, and little wind bedeviled them. The cows were in no immediate danger of exposure or starvation, as the snow remained powdery enough for them to scrape through to the cured grass beneath.

Morgan's range encompassed the better part of ten square miles on either side of the milky river, a good bit of territory to cover. In the first few days they'd discover clumps of several dozen cows, usually in the vicinity of the water, hurrah them into sluggish motion, and walk them back to the stockyards. Later the subherds grew smaller, animals that had wandered farther afield.

By week's end Morgan was able to report a count of 270 animals in the pens, thirty-four less than he'd turned out the previous spring. But he would be satisfied, he told them, if they could search up another dozen or so; inevitably there would be losses to predators, disease, and the recent rustling.

They saw no sign of the Indians, nor of any other mortal. This might have been attributable to Holt's and Sam's presence, but in the normal course of their activities, the wolfers should be gone by now, Morgan explained during one supper in response to Sam's inquiry.

The bounty offered by the Stockgrowers Association was three dollars a pelt, but the profit did not end there. Once shown as proof, the wolfer was allowed to sell the fur for whatever it might fetch him. A nice thick specimen would bring another six or seven dollars from the traders at Fort Benton—and winter was the season when coats were the most luxuriant and wolves most easy to track.

Winter also meant the suspension of river navigation as the sluggish Missouri iced up, so pelts could not be shipped. For expediency, the successful wolfer left his victims' carcasses to freeze. Each hunter had a mark, a crude brand registered with Quint, which was carved with a knife into the wolf's cheek. When thaw arrived with spring, the animals were skinned, the pelts were hauled out, and finally carted to Benton, where the fur traders arrived on the first steamboats after the ice broke up.

What this meant for the nonce was that, by now, the wolfers would be spread out over the high country. Some might come into Lobo once a month or so, for provisions and to enjoy the rude amenities, but others stayed in the outback for the duration, sleeping under buffalo robes and eating a diet of jerky and occasional fresh elk, supplemented with just enough camas root to keep scurvy from loosening their teeth.

Gutt, if he was among them, would be a lot harder to find than a few strays. That was the thought in Holt's mind when Sam reined abruptly, shot him a glance and put a forefinger to her lips.

They'd crested a knoll, and beyond its foot, a half mile distant, a dozen or so cows were moving slowly north. Five riders on unsaddled horses were harrying them on. Holt made out long braids descending from beneath the flat brims of round-crowned hats.

"I'll be dipped," Holt said. "At least Morgan was talking straight about one thing." He thumped the bay. "Come on."

Sam caught up as Holt descended the rise. "You wouldn't think I was meddling if I pointed something out?"

"Be my guest."

"We're outnumbered. You figure to just ride up and ask them to give those cows back?"

"Yup. With Indians this is like a game. If they get caught, they lose, and no one is supposed to hold a grudge. They'll be peaceable enough."

One of the rustlers spotted them and raised a cry. The others reined up. "See?" Holt said. "I know Indians."

"Good for you," Sam said, and threw herself forward on the neck of her roan.

Holt peered through the snow and saw that three of them had drawn rifles.

"Duck, you idiot," Sam said.

Holt took the advice a second before a bullet whistled somewhere over their heads.

"This is crazy," Holt said. "No Indian would chance killing a white man over cows."

"Fine," Sam said. "So let's continue on in and pow-wow."

Another shot rang out, although the idea seemed not so much to hit them as to drive them off. Given that Holt didn't plan to try gunning them down, it looked like it would work—

Close by, a rifle went off.

Holt whirled the bay in time to see Charity Morgan levering another cartridge into the chamber of her Winchester. "Put up that long gun," he ordered.

"We've got the chance to catch them." Charity was a bit out of breath. "Prove once and for all that the Blackfeet are innocent. These aren't them—I'm sure of it."

Holt remembered the Indian with whom she appeared a few days previous, but now was neither the time for questions nor foolhardy derring-do. He wrenched the rifle from her.

So he was off balance as the rustlers fired a third time, and Holt's bay took advantage. It fishtailed around, tossing Holt into the snow, and then cantered off.

Holt made his feet, put Sam's horse between him and the gunmen. "I guess we'll back off."

"Good guess," Sam said acridly.

"Climb back so I can take the saddle."

"I'll keep the saddle, thank you very much," Sam snapped. "You can ride behind."

Argument seemed futile. Holt handed her Charity's gun and swung aboard, compelled to hold Sam by the waist. She backed the roan away, Charity following. In a few minutes they were out of range but still in sightline, could see the rustlers move on with spoils.

Holt's bay was waiting on the other side of the knoll. Before they reached him, Sam said sarcastically, " 'I know Indians.' Humpf."

Holt slid off and retrieved the bay. "Do me a favor and keep this whole episode to yourself," he requested. "I been embarrassed enough lately."

Charity rode up, luminous with anger and the crazy look she could put on or take off like a coat. "You embarrassed me," she snapped. "Give me back my rifle, and don't meddle ever again, unless you want me to demonstrate what real meddling is about."

Holt ignored her and got rehorsed.

"I know who you are," Charity said ominously, "and I know what you are worth to the law."

Holt gaped at her. "Morgan," he breathed. "That dog-eared son of a bitch."

"Maybe I'll keep it to myself," Charity said. "But for sure you are going to return my gun."

Sam did so.

Charity took it and laughed, wheeled her horse and rode off at a quick trot.

Holt stared at her back. He could have cheerfully bound her in a burlap bag and dropped it down a well.

Nor would he hesitate to add Morgan for good measure.

Chapter Seven

Holt's brooding would not abate, and was profound enough that Sam let him be for the next few hours. "I'm going to fix his wagon," Holt said as they crossed one of the ditches that flowed from the milky river.

"You're feeling melancholia," Sam suggested.

"Melancholia is when you are blue for no reason."

"How did you know that?"

Holt turned his glare on her. "I'm not completely unlettered," he said. "As for Morgan—"

"Morgan is playing a double game with us. Maybe he told Charity our story, maybe not."

"How else would she know?"

"We'll come to learn that. Meanwhile there is no advantage to revealing our hand."

Holt returned to his morose silence. This far north and this close to the winter solstice, the rate at which the days grew shorter was quickening, and this one had never been that bright to begin with.

When they stumbled on the cows around four o'clock, the first tinge of twilight was already darkening the eastern sky.

That they found them at all was dumb luck on the cows' part. They were by the river and hidden by thicket, and Holt and Sam would have rode right past if one of the animals had not lowed miserably. They backtracked, followed a trace of path down to the water, and found four pairs of mothers and heifers, with Morgan's SM brand on their flanks.

Holt stared at them sourly. "When the good Lord handed out common sense, I reckon cows were last in line."

At this point in the stream, Morgan had thrown up a diversion dam to feed the ditch and form a watering tank that stretched about twenty-five yards upstream and down- from where the cows milled disconsolately. There the placid water had frozen over, and although there was open flow above them, this is where the cows always drank, and this by God was where they expected to drink now.

"If these bovines had the sense to move to where the water is," Holt said, "they wouldn't have moaned in frustration and we'd not have found them. Let's run them in."

He unloosed his riata from the saddle horn to hurrah the animals away from the stream, and in the time that took, one of the heifers walked out on the ice.

"Aw hell." Holt whistled sharply.

The animal ignored him, took two more steps, and plunged through the fragile surface.

The cow sunk only up to the hocks, a yard or so from the bank. But that was deep enough to make climbing back out on its own impossible, and from the wild rolling look in its eyes, it was about to panic.

Holt swung down, slung the rope around his neck, rolled up the legs of his britches and union suit, and drew his Colt.

"You going to shoot it?" Sam asked, incredulous.

Holt didn't waste breath on an answer. "There's a wool sweater in my saddlebag. Dig it out and cut it in half, front and back." He unloaded the gun and pocketed the cartridges, knowing this was not going to be pleasant.

He broke through the ice on his first step, which he expected; he was heavier than the heifer and his weight distributed on two feet only. He bent, pounded at the surface with the butt of his pistol. It gave way to allow him another step.

It was necessary to repeat the process another half-dozen times before he reached the more open water around the cow. By now his boots were full and he stood knee deep in the frigid water.

"You all right?" Sam called.

"Yeah, but I figure I got about ninety more seconds if I want to keep all my toes."

The other seven cows were safe for now, content to drink from the bank at the water Holt had opened. He holstered the gun, freed the loop from the coil of rope, set a gentling hand on the heifer's flank to divert its attention, and dropped the noose over its head and around its neck.

The cow followed meekly as Holt waded back to shore. He continued until they were fifty feet from the water, the other cows trailing amiably along.

Holt sat on a deadfall tree trunk, yanked off his boots and socks. "The sweater. Also, cut a couple of three-foot lengths of rope."

The skin of his feet was wrinkled and fish-belly white, but as he carefully dried them with his neckerchief, he discovered no dots of purer white that meant frostbite. He took the rope and bolts of wool that had been his sweater and used them to fashion a pair of booties, then got remounted quick as he could.

The cows' luck must have extended to him: they reached Morgan's cabin in less than a half hour and a few minutes before full dark. Holt insisted on penning the animals before seeing to other business. He felt the cold ground through the wool of his makeshift footgear.

"You saved it," Sam said.

Holt closed the corral gate. "That's me," he muttered. "Guardian of all the Lord's creatures."

Holt sat by the stove with his feet in a washbasin of steaming water, enjoying the sensation of feeling returning to his toes. His frozen boots were cooking near the stove, and Sam returned from the bunkhouse with dry socks as Holt finished telling Morgan about the rustlers.

As Morgan splashed whiskey into a tumbler and handed it to Holt, Prospect entered, shook snow from the shoulders of his coat. "I blanketed and grained your animals." Holt said thanks. He'd wanted to see to it himself, but Sam insisted that for the moment the horses were in less need than he.

Prospect watched Holt drink, looked thirstily at the bottle in Morgan's hand. Morgan shook his head slightly. "We've got 278 head in now," Prospect said, "and in the nick of time. It looks like some real weather is fixing to blow."

The stove fire was drafting with vigor, and Holt could hear the wind whistling past the well-chinked house. This was not the best of conditions for manhunting, but with the cows gathered, Gutt was next on his agenda....

"So you did nothing," Morgan declared abruptly.

Holt accepted a cigarette from Sam. "Beg pardon?" She struck a match on the seat of her pants, and he dipped the tip of his smoke into it.

"You had rifles," Morgan said. "You could have returned fire."

"They weren't trying to kill us, only drive us off."

"That didn't take much."

Holt drank to give himself time to come up with a temperate response. He settled on, "Whatever you say."

"They were burdened with the cows," Morgan said. "If you circled around, you could have picked them off."

That was sufficient needle. "I don't backshoot," Holt said. "I've been backshot myself."

Morgan regarded him. "Perhaps such an experience unsettled your nerve."

"Listen to yourself," Holt said to Morgan. "You're telling me you wished an Indian war."

"Long as someone else was fighting it for you," Sam added.

Morgan reddened. "At least you could have followed them."

"We were in unfamiliar territory in what could pass for the dead of winter," Holt said, trying to remain reasonable. "I'm not about to be caught out after dark, nor risk spending the night lost, miserable, and exposed."

He finished what was in his glass, held it out. Morgan ignored him. "Plus," Holt went on, "you seem to forget we had a deal. I've gathered your cows—and by the way, we could have just as easily missed those last eight. That sort of makes up for the ones we lost."

"Is that how you see it?"

"Now that we're done, we've got someone to find, as you well know," Sam picked up.

"Those rustlers could still be tracked."

Sam gestured at the window, where wind was packing snow into the corners of the panes. "In that?"

Morgan clearly did not like taking this from a woman, but there wasn't anything to be done about it now. Holt felt silly sitting like an invalid in a footbath, and his boots looked to be dry. He donned the clean socks and pulled them on. Prospect removed the basin, opened the front door long enough to admit snow and chill wind while he dumped the water, then went into the kitchen. Uncomfortable silence occupied the cabin for a quarter hour, until Prospect reappeared to announce that supper was served.

Holt studied the cards in his hand, glanced at Sam's five of spades on the table, and played the king. Prospect Morgan dropped the ace atop it and raked in the trick to win the hand. The game was euchre. Prospect wet the tip of a pencil on his tongue and recorded the score.

"I have always been good at cards," he said absently, "except for three games—monte, faro, and poker, the ones where a man can make money." He pushed the pad to one side, began to shuffle. "A metaphor for my fortune in general."

He dealt. A couple hours earlier, after the supper of ham and boiled potatoes, Prospect entered the bunkhouse carrying a quart bottle of bourbon with an inch gone and his breath betraying its disposition.

He appeared to have concerns on his mind, as did Holt. If Charity knew who he and Sam were, it was a good bet that Prospect did as well. "Your daughter," Holt had said as they settled at the table, "has bandied words about us."

"To me, principally," Prospect said.

"I guessed it was the other way around."

Prospect shook his head. "My brother keeps a diary. Charity has a habit of snooping."

"Swell," Holt said. "Why wasn't she at supper?"

"She never came back this evening." Prospect didn't seem at all concerned.

"Where is she?" Sam asked.

Prospect dealt the first hand. "With the Blackfeet," he said. Holt remembered the Indian with whom she'd been riding a few days earlier. "Or in town," Prospect continued.

"Sweller yet," Holt had said sourly.

Now it was around ten o'clock and the bottle was half empty, with Prospect responsible for downing most of it. He sorted his cards.

"A year ago I had a half-section homestead outside Ely, Minnesota," he said. "Two hundred acres in red wheat, better than another hundred in feed oats. It would never make me rich, but we made out good enough, the missus and me." He led a low heart. "That winter was not destined to treat me with kindness."

Sam won with the queen. Prospect nodded complacently, as if she was playing into his hand. "The week before Christmas, the missus took sick with a cold. By the holiday double pneumonia had settled into her lungs. She didn't live to see the new year."

"I'm sorry," Sam murmured.

"She was only forty," Prospect said, "but she had worked hard as any man for half a lifetime, and it caught up with her. That's just the craziness of fate, but what happened next was due to the craziness of people."

Prospect lost the second trick, again to Sam, then went up on her lead with an ace. "Three years before her ma died, Charity had left the farm for a convent school in Chicago. Neither me nor the missus were comfortable with her going off at such an age, but we reckoned the nuns would see that no harm came to her. Probably they would have."

He followed the ace with the king of spades, and Sam and Holt both showed out of the suit. Prospect dropped the rest of his cards on the table face up—they were all spades—and claimed the rest of the tricks.

"It turned out that she left the convent after two weeks." He jotted down his score and added figures, but did not pick up the deck to redeal. "We had no way of knowing. We wrote to her and she replied on their stationery. She has ways of managing such stunts."

"What was she really doing?"

"She says she was working as a salesgirl in Field's department store." Prospect shrugged. "It could be the truth. Somehow she managed to save up near a thousand dollars."

He poured a drink, gestured with the bottle. Sam shook her head, but Holt decided he'd have one more.

"I wired her about her mother's death," Prospect said. "I got no reply, but three days later she showed up at the farm to stay. When spring came, she would work in her mother's stead, she told me, and I accepted. I could not afford to hire any hands, nor could I farm the place myself."

A loose windowpane rattled in the wind. Sam got up and fed the stove another chunk of cordwood. "We got on more than decently. She wasn't as you've seen her, though she was willful, but she did no real harm, and I had no choice but to put up with her ways."

"Willful how?" Sam asked.

"She couldn't bear spending the winter cooped up in that cabin—hell, it was never easy on me and the missus, either. Charity would go into town when the weather permitted. I knew she had a beau." Prospect reddened. "Sometimes she spent the night."

"That's nothing for you to be ashamed of," Sam said.

Prospect shook his head. "What I'm ashamed of, telling you this story, is my real motive, which was basic selfishness. I feared she'd get in a family way and be unable to work once planting season arrived."

That seemed practical to Holt, and he said so.

"Winter lingered and the weather didn't break until mid-April. I did take the wagon into town then, for seed and gear and to get some equipment repaired. Charity came with me. We'd both be spending the night this time, while the smithy fixed up a harrow of mine.

"We took separate rooms, of course," Prospect said. "Around midnight she came into mine, sobbing uncontrollably. Her eye was blackened and her face bruised, and her nightclothes were torn. She said she'd been—" Prospect hesitated. "—abused in other ways as well.

"A doctor came, saw to her, and gave her a sleeping potion, so I didn't learn details until morning. It turned out that her beau was one Horace Landusky. I knew the name; it was attached to one of the wealthiest and most influential families in Ely. Horace was the scion, a young man about Charity's age."

A knot exploded in the stove and sparks flew through the grate and blinked out. "She admitted that they were intimate, although she had taken precautions. But a few weeks earlier, she had ended the relationship. Landusky became inflamed; thus the assault."

"You went to the authorities," Sam guessed.

"And were dismissed out of hand," Prospect confirmed. "The weight of prejudice and influence was stacked against us. Charity had been with this Landusky for months; he was of good stock while we were dirt farmers; in fact, Charity's attractiveness was used to suggest that she had egged him on. No charges would be brought."

Prospect drank. "Her mood grew dark over the next few weeks. She would rise from depression to manic activity, even cheerfulness, and then descend once more. I feared for her sanity." He stared off past them. "I had reason to fear, but not for that," he added cryptically.

"She returned to town several times, demonstrating her mania in public. She stood in the midst of the street weeping. She entered saloons where women were not permitted, and demanded drink. Once she took another's horse and paraded up and down the street on it. In short, she became a public nuisance."

Sam had evidently figured something out that had eluded Holt. "It was an act."

While Holt was chewing on that, Prospect said, "Probably. Even I don't know." He wiped his chin with the back of his hand, which shook a bit, from emotion or the liquor he'd consumed. "One day she returned to Ely for the last time."

The storm was waxing; the cabin's walls fairly shook in the wind. "The Landusky family lived in a mansion on the north edge of town. What happened next I know only from piecing together information.

"Charity strode into the house without knocking. The Landuskys—the wealthy capitalist, his wife, and young Horace—were taking supper. Charity carried a pistol in one hand and an axe handle in the other."

Holt felt a sense of dread, as if the scene were unfolding before him.

"She held them at bay, ordering Horace to his knees. When he complied, she went to work with the club. It is a wonder she did not kill him. As it was, she broke his right arm and left leg so badly that they would never work right again."

"Jesus God," Holt exhaled.

Prospect sighed heavily. "In the end she was arrested, there in the dining room of the mansion and splattered with blood, babbling incoherently." He glanced at Sam. "This, too, was likely playacting. In the aftermath, she was charged with assault, judged mentally incompetent to stand trial, and we were forced out of town at gunpoint. What happened to our property I've no idea."

"You can't blame her," Sam said.

"Blame was irrelevant," Prospect pointed out. "We wandered until her money ran out, and then we came here to beg my brother's benevolence."

He was beginning to slur his words, and when he picked up the deck once more and attempted to shuffle, the cards squirted between his fingers and across the table. "I suppose this game is over." He consulted the score sheet. "Between the two of you, I'm owed sixty-seven cents."

Holt dug a silver dollar from his pocket, balanced it on edge, and set it to spinning with a flick of his finger. The three of them watched until it wavered and toppled. "What does she know about this man that we seek?" Holt asked as he watched the coin clatter to a stop.

"Ask her. Maybe you can talk to her—I sure as hell cannot." Prospect planted his hands on the table. "I'm soused," he announced.

As he attempted to stand, Holt rose and lunged for a grab of Prospect's shirtfront. He missed. Prospect fell away and knocked over his chair to tumble to the floor, where he began to snore contentedly.

"Now there's an idea," Holt said with heavy irony. "Get ourselves some shut-eye."

"What do we do with him?"

Holt wrestled Prospect over his shoulder, staggered under his weight to the far bunk, and dumped him upon it. As an afterthought he drew the blanket around him; it would be chill in this bunkhouse by morning. "Bedtime for everyone," he said roughly to Sam. "Tomorrow figures to be a long day."

"What's our plan?"

"I ponder better when the sun is up," Holt said. "If there is any sun."

They washed in silence and undressed behind the privacy of the blanket. With Prospect as their unexpected guest, Holt was compelled, to his consternation, to move one cot closer to the barrier.

Sam, damn her eyes, knew his thoughts exactly. He doused the lantern, damped down the stove, and climbed under the covers.

Her tone was rich with teasing. "Nighty-night," she said softly.

Chapter Eight

Holt awoke in dimness, in response not so much to noise, but to a sense of something changed, a subtle shift in his surroundings. As he came fully around, he did hear a sound, of a horse snorting in the barnyard.

He pulled on his pants and jacket, took the Colt from where it lay holstered in the vacant adjacent bunk. Despite the days of hard physical labor, he'd slept lightly each night, hoping that the departure of Quint's wolfers would stay his hand, but alert all the same to any surreptitious intrusion by the Lobo town boss.

The bunk where he'd dumped Prospect was empty. Sam stirred as Holt opened the door, said, "What?"

Holt went cautiously out. It felt close to dawn, but except for a faint streak of lighter sky off east, the darkness was dense. Near the stock pens a rider dismounted. "Who goes there?" Holt demanded.

The rider led the horse toward him, and Holt made out it was Charity.

"What the hell are you doing about at this hour?" Holt snapped.

"Helping you." Charity rubbed her gloved hands. "I've had a cold ride."

"Come on," Holt said.

Inside, Sam was up and dressing. Holt turned quickly away, busied himself making a fire. He caught Charity watching him with vague amusement. "You were in Lobo?" he guessed.

"Yes."

WINTER OF THE WOLF 57

Holt felt testy, from lack of sleep, coffee, and peace of mind, and this girl knowing all about him and now back from a pleasant sojourn with the genial Mr. Quint. "I'd expect you'd choose your company more carefully," he said meanly, "after what happened to you in Ely."

"Holt," Sam said in reproach. She tucked in her shirt, went to get the pot and coffee.

Charity's expression was neutral, though, and her manner unaffected. It was the first time Holt had seen her absent of any hint of mania. "I knew my father would tell."

Holt muttered an apology.

"Here is my side of the story," Charity went on. "As to my years in Chicago, my father simply won't accept the truth. I was chaste, working as a shopgirl and attending Lakeside College of Commerce and Industry at night. If my mother hadn't died, I'd have graduated in another term."

"Why pretend to be at the convent?" Sam asked.

"I was young, and I thought my parents would object if they knew that I'd decided the religious life was not for me. It was one of those lies that once told, entraps you. No harm was done."

Charity turned to Holt. "But that's not what you wanted to know."

"None of my business," Holt grunted.

"I was indeed sleeping with Horace Landusky," she went on, "and it had nothing to do with his money or station. I was in love with him. Later I realized that made two of us, since Horace was in love only with himself and his money."

Sam set the pot on the boil, watching Charity with interest.

"When I broke it off, he ranted and railed. He didn't give a fig about me, but his maleness had been sullied. His response was to brutally rape me."

"But before that—"

"Do yourself a favor, Holt," Sam cut in. "Shut your trap."

"That we were previously intimate is irrelevant," Charity

said patiently. "This had nothing to do with sex and everything to do with violation."

Holt took Sam's advice.

"Afterward, it's possible I really was a little crazy," Charity said, "but most of it was part of my plan. Horace was the criminal deserving of punishment, not I, but the law took his side. Pretending insanity was the only way I could think of to protect myself after . . . after I'd done what I had to."

Charity looked a bit rueful. "I didn't foresee the loss of my father's farm. That I regret—but only that."

The coffeepot began to steam, and Sam added grounds. The cabin grew warmer by degrees.

"I learned defenses, so I would never fear a man again," Charity said. "My make-believe mania is one, and I showed it to you when you first arrived, and since. I am in a tenuous enough situation here as it is, and I wanted to be sure how you affected it. Until then it was best you believed I was lunatic."

Holt breathed in the revivifying aroma of the brewing java. "So," he said carefully, "how do we affect your situation?"

"I love my father," Charity said, "but you see how he is. Being forced to ask his brother for a roof and sustenance was one blow, and the tension of this present conflict is another. The drinking has never been this bad, and if something isn't done to resolve the issue—to banish his fears—I will lose him.

"And I respect my uncle," she continued. "I want you to make his holdings secure again, by stopping the threat of Quint. Lastly, I know you must find this Gutt, I know why, and now that I've made my decision, I wish to aid you."

"Was the part about you sneaking a look at Morgan's diary the truth?"

"Yes," Charity said, with no apology in her tone. "Like everything else I do, I thought it was to all of our benefit."

"Including going into town last night," Holt surmised. "What did you tell Quint?"

"Nothing." But Charity looked a bit guilty. "I talked to Emma."

Sam gave her an inquiring look.

"Emma Franks is Quint's woman," Charity explained. "She was in Fort Benton arranging for supplies when you and Quint had your run-in."

"All right," Holt said. "What did you tell this Emma woman?"

Sam poured coffee and gave Charity a cup. She sipped at it and appeared to veer off course. "When I go to town, I put on my act and watch and listen, my uncle's eyes and ears. I've seen Gutt."

There was a frisson in her tone that Holt understood, recalling his one interview with the big man in a driving rainstorm on the plains of southern Utah. He had never expected to leave it alive.

"A wolfer accosted me. I put him off firmly, but it was late in the day and others were drunk and began to egg him on. I saw myself in the center of what was about to become a mob with a mob's mentality, the suspension of any shreds of decent behavior to which they might have individually clung."

She drank again, stared into the cup. "Gutt interceded. He grabbed two fistfuls of the back of the wolfer's coat and carried him across the bar to the door as if he were a sack of laundry. He used the wolfer's head to swing open the doors and tossed him out into the road." She smiled. "Nobody took exception, and Gutt spoke not a word, hardly looked at me." She regarded Holt. "He cannot be all bad."

"No one is, but he comes close." Holt recalled something else. "What was that nonsense yesterday about turning us in yourself?"

"Idle chatter," Charity said. "As to your other question, I told Emma nothing, but I did ask where Gutt was."

Holt accepted coffee. "And she was pleased to answer."

"No," Charity said.

Holt felt like throwing up his hands.

"But I found out," Charity went on. "The way the

wolfing works is something like mining claims, with Quint the arbitrator. He divides up the country and assigns it by lot, various wolfers taking to each of the drainages. Few break the bargain; the last who did was mistaken for an elk and gut-shot—accidentally, of course."

Charity smiled wanly. "Until you came, I was the only other woman in these parts, and Emma tolerates me. Last night I slept in the bar, as I have before. In the back room are ledger books, kept by Emma. Quint can't read, write, nor cipher.

"One of the books," Charity said, "lists the assigned territories. I found it early this morning, and then Quint found me."

Holt felt a sinking sensation. "So you were compelled to tell him what you were doing, and for us?"

Charity shook her head. "He'd never molest me. Emma wouldn't stand for it."

Holt wondered exactly what that meant, but left the question for later.

"Gutt's wolfing territory is up the draw defined by a stream called Rock Creek," Charity said. "My uncle has a map—or I could guide you."

"Thanks, but no," Holt said automatically. His thoughts had shifted, to Fate once again moving him about like a chess piece. The plan he'd claimed to be working on the night before was all pretend, which didn't matter, because yet again, the next step had been made for him.

He studied Sam. "I guess I'll be heading up there, then."

"*We,*" she corrected, "and don't waste your breath arguing." Sam turned to Charity. "Thanks for your help."

Holt was feeling a bit more ambiguous about Charity's "help," but held his peace. He finished his coffee, closed the damper on the stove.

"I reckon it's time to head for the hills," he said.

Stanley Morgan, if not completely pleased, was upstanding about his end of the bargain. After breakfast he outfitted them with gear and provisions: ammunition, blankets, thick robes to wear over their jackets, and enough food to last them the better part of a week, though Holt hoped this little winter camp-out wouldn't take near as long. Morgan didn't solicit their promise to return, but was conspicuously unforthcoming with any wages owed, the sort of ambiguous behavior Holt was learning to expect from the rancher.

Prospect was more displeased with their departure, and moody with apprehension as he served the morning meal. At one point he said to his brother, "You might have to start thinking about making a deal."

Morgan scowled at him. "A man does not deal with snakes."

Prospect met his gaze. "A man could get snakebit just the same."

When they set out at mid-morning, Holt's ears burned with the cold, and the day's progress did not much ameliorate it. By the time they reached the milky river, they were riding through unusual gloom even for this season. The sky was a perfect canopy of unbroken overcast, and even the snow at their feet seemed grayish.

Holt wrapped the robe more closely around him and took a few tentative steps upon the ice that covered one of the river's pools. In this deep freeze, it did not bend a whit under his weight. He walked the bay across without mishap, gestured for Sam to follow. Back in the saddle he said abruptly, "Just because I didn't make objection doesn't mean you're not one more thing I got to worry about."

"Not true," Sam said firmly.

As usual, Holt thought dismally, he'd put his foot in it. He pressed on. "I'm in a mess through no choice. That doesn't go for you."

"Here is something I have learned: everything a person does in life is a matter of choice, and only fools deny it. You chose to go into law work, you chose to get involved with Cat Lacey, and you chose to be drunk the night Gutt killed her."

Holt gasped.

"I'm not accusing you of anything," Sam said. "I'm stating facts. You also chose to go along with my plan to bust you out, and to accept my help in clearing your name."

"And you?"

"I choose to set my own rules. Always have, plan to continue in the future."

Holt worked on a response. "I'm doing my best to come to terms with that."

"You've more experience than I with this sort of business," Sam said. "But don't put undue emphasis on that. What we have in common is the need to find Gutt, and that we're both scared at the prospect. Only way to face that fear is together."

This reminded Holt of his mixed emotions when he was on the bronco at Brantville's rodeo, once the whistle blew: relief mixed with apprehension. In an effort to move his thoughts along, he said, "You trust Charity?"

"I don't distrust her." Sam dwelled on the question. "She as much as admitted she had an agenda."

"I wouldn't mind knowing what it is," Holt said.

"She asked this Emma woman about Gutt," Sam said, reasoning it out. "Likely she wasn't inquiring on her own account, which leaves us. Add to that, Quint failed to drive you away." Sam made a sour face. "I'd say the seeds of suspicion are sown."

To the south Holt could make out the blot on the prairie that was the settlement of Lobo, as they gave it a berth of at least a mile. Holt gazed at the town, shook his head as if denying some comment of Sam's. "We've done what we promised Morgan. Now is the time to get Gutt and finish our business."

Sam was peering off toward the mountains to the west.

"I believe that in the end Charity's loyalties lie with her uncle," Holt said. "Her visit to town might have gained information that benefits us, or she may have known it all along. But as you said, now Quint and this Emma know we are after Gutt, and will be pondering on the why of it. Charity might have wished this to happen."

"For what reason?"

"Same reason as Morgan," Holt said. "Pit us against Quint and hope he loses."

Sam reined up, pointed ahead of them. "Could be it worked," she said.

Quint caressed the knuckles of his right hand over the steel plate of his jaw, the gesture almost tender. "Here is what I wonder," he said. "Why do you still pollute my territory?"

The woman who sat horseback at his side gave him a schoolmarmish stare, turned it on Holt and then Sam. She'd be Emma Franks, Holt reckoned. A somewhat rank-smelling buffalo robe hung limply and open to reveal a gaunt, chestless frame swimming within. Wiry hair the color of the inside of a tin can frizzed out from beneath a cloth cap with earflaps. Her features were plain and angular, sharp blades of chinbone and a hawkish nose above thin, tightly pursed lips.

"I know you two," she said ominously.

Holt nodded politely and waited to see how much trouble that comment boded.

But Emma only said, "You are of a type. What do you want with Gutt?"

Quint and Emma had spotted them from no more than fifty feet when they emerged from the brush along the river, so it had been too late to run even if they wished to. Holt did not. He was tired of giving up control of his activities to the whims of others. "I owe him money," Holt answered.

"Sure you do," Quint said. "Give it over and I'll see that he gets it. Your welcome is wore out in these parts."

Holt met his gaze. "Yeah, I remember that welcome. Maybe you and me'll have the chance to finish that business."

Holt was mildly surprised that Quint didn't come back with some threatening rejoinder. Emma snapped at him, "I'll conduct this interview, and let you know when you are needed." She stared him down. "Assuming you are up to the job."

Quint looked away and rubbed vigorously at the steel plate, as if polishing it. Whatever was going on, Emma wore, or at least shared, the pants in this partnership. That was middling strange.

"There is business here that is none of yours," Emma said, "business that will work itself out in time and without meddling. We let you bring in Morgan's cows. Maybe we were doing you a favor, maybe you served our purpose. Now you are not needed." She nodded at Quint, as if giving a permission.

"You recall that beating I gave you?" he asked.

"Vividly," Holt said.

Quint ignored Holt's ironic tone. "It's nothing compared to what I'll do if I see you after today. I'll break so many bones you'll have to hire someone to pick your nose for you."

"No," Sam said.

Holt glanced over. Her buffalo robe had parted, and she held her gun at a point between Emma and Quint.

Emma ignored her in favor of a long second look at Holt. Something glimmered in her dull dark eyes. Sam waggled the revolver without getting Emma's attention, though Quint kept his eye on her.

"You are digging your own grave," Emma said to Holt, "in more ways than you know. Why should I not let you?"

Holt saw Quint quiver in the saddle, as if ready to make a move but apprehensive at the results. Sam fired over his head and Quint stopped moving.

Paying not the slightest attention and never taking her eyes from Holt, Emma Franks reached over and backhanded Quint across his good cheek. "Put your hands out in sight," she ordered.

This episode was veering in bizarre directions, Holt thought. He recalled Quint before the fight was forced in the bar the previous week, his sense that despite the man's size and reputation, some little mouse of fear was in permanent residence in his mental framework.

"More ways than you know," Emma repeated, as if the

conversation had never been interrupted, "starting with how you likely won't come out of those mountains except belly down."

She turned her horse toward town, oblivious to the gun Sam still held. Quint followed.

Emma looked back over her shoulder. "But if you happen to get lucky, we'll pick up where we left off. Nothing I like better than a good chitchat."

Chapter Nine

It was mid-afternoon by the time they reached the Rocky Mountain Front, so-called because in the old days the east side of the range marked wagon-train immigrants' first sight of the awesome obstacle that stood between them and the Promised Land. The front also took its name from the abrupt way the prairie turned to steep mountain, as if in some prehistoric time the earth had buckled, squeezed, and exploded upward. "They're awe-inspiring," Sam said.

"And forboding, in more ways than one." Much like the encounter with Quint and Emma, he thought, which had posed more questions than it answered. "Why'd she have that abrupt change of heart?"

A narrow valley cut by a creek provided entrée to the mountains just ahead. Sam looked from it to Holt. "I've figured out the gist of your problem," she said. "Antecedents."

"Huh?"

"You jump right into old issues pronoun-first, without any clue to what they refer."

"That Emma woman, of course," Holt said impatiently.

"I don't know," Sam replied to the first question. "Clearly she is the brains of that duo, and figured that setting us loose to seek Gutt was to her advantage. I doubt she does anything that isn't."

"Let's worry about immediate dangers," Holt suggested. "Like wolfers in general and Gutt in particular."

Sam was willing to drop it as well. "The grizzlies will be hibernating by now, at least. I did a story about them."

WINTER OF THE WOLF 67

"Then you didn't do your homework," Holt said. "Griz do sleep most of the winter, but it's not true hibernation. They'll even get up and roam around once in a while." He laughed suddenly. "That reminds me of a tale."

He dug out the tracing of Morgan's map he'd made, and on which he'd jotted notes. "When I was a kid and we were living down south of here, the only other folks in the near vicinity were ranchers a half-dozen miles away. There was a son my age named Billy Jenks, and we got to be pals."

He unfolded the map and smoothed it. "About the only season I got time to play was winter, and even then there wasn't much of it, between chores. But this one occasion, I got my father to let me go with Billy on a camp-out in the mountains. I told him I'd bring back an elk, but mostly it was for the adventure of it. I fancied myself the incarnation of John Colter."

"Who's John Colter?"

"Mountain man who'd been with Lewis and Clark. He spent six months of the winter of 1808 traipsing not far from where we ended up living, carrying nothing but a buffalo robe, a rifle, a skinning knife, and coffee. Billy'd lent me a book about him.

"Anyhow," Holt said, "when we make camp, it turns out Billy swiped a jug of homemade beer from his old man. We're all of fourteen at the time, so naturally we drink the jug dry, and naturally Billy has to go to the bushes. A minute later he comes racing back, all excited."

Holt watched the static clouds touching at the mountains' crowns. "He's stumbled across a grizzly den, a hollow clawed out around the roots of a big fallen Doug fir. He dares me to come look, which of course means I got to do it."

"Plus by then you've got a bellyful of liquid courage."

"Right. We're standing about ten feet away, and Billy whispers, 'It's hibernating. When they're hibernating, it's like they're dead. Nothing'll wake them.'

"So I say, 'Fine, but if you think I'm spending the night

within shouting distance of this behemoth'—it must have weighed four hundred pounds easy—'you are loco. Let's go move camp.'

"Billy says, 'It can't wake up even if it wants to,' and before I can press my side of the argument, he says, 'For two bits, I'd go up and kick it.' "

Holt shook his head. "If aiding and abetting idiocy were a crime when you're fourteen, I'd be a felon. Because me and the homebrew say, 'I'd pay two bits to see that.'

"Billy looks a mite green, not expecting me to take him up, but two bits is a lot of money and there's his grit at stake. He hitches up his britches, takes a deep breath, walks up to the bruin, and nudges it with his toe.

"I say, 'That's no kick.' Billy curses, rears back, and boots the bear in the ribs with all his might."

"Thereby, I'm guessing, conclusively disproving his hibernation theories," Sam said.

"I should hope to shout. The bear lets out this roar of surprise, looks up to see this fool standing over him, swipes at him with a set of claws the size of a dinner plate."

"I've heard that God watches over drunks and small children," Sam said, "and since you and Billy were both, I'm hoping this story has an amusing ending."

"We each made it to a tree. We couldn't have gone up them faster if someone had lit off dynamite under our butts. The bear hung around for what seemed like half the night, while we clung on, shivered, and stayed enough scared not to fall asleep.

"Here's the punch line," Holt said. "When we got back—and I did get an elk, by the way—I stiffed Billy on the two bits. So he threatens to kick the stuffing out of me, and I say if he tries it, I'll tell his dad about the homebrew he filched."

"That was a nasty trick," Sam observed.

"Billy felt the same way," Holt said, "but he got over it."

Sam pointed at the map. "I can't help but notice that we've sort of drifted away from our original purpose. We were talking about dangers."

"I was thinking back to what Charity said about the divvying up of the wolfing territory. We could be seen as claim jumpers, and there's an honored doctrine of shoot first, ask questions later on that count."

"Oh my goodness. We'd better turn back right this minute." She was being sarcastic. "You're stalling. Why?"

He ignored the question in favor of studying the map and his notes. A quarter mile back they'd crossed a ten-foot-wide creek with water the same milky color of Morgan's river; Holt figured it was a tributary. Rock Creek in turn flowed into it, by the chart he was studying. The landmarks at the point where it exited the mountains were a six-foot-high falls with a pool behind it, the gallows frame of an abandoned mine shaft upslope from its left-bank bench, and a cliff of painted rocks opposite.

Sam looked over his shoulder. "This is it," she decided. "Why are the rocks all those colors?"

"Minerals, pyrites and such. Do I look like a geologist?"

"No, you look like a man of two minds." She pointed left and right. "There's the falls, there's the shaft. Let's get moving."

This would have been pretty country under other circumstances, but Holt was in a mood. All the time they had been tracking Gutt, ever since Sam had broken him out of Yuma, he'd had the nagging feeling he was like a mongrel chasing a stagecoach: If the cur did catch up, what did it mean to do with it?

The drainage defined by Rock Creek, according to the map, did not become impassable canyon until just below its headwaters. In the lower reaches it was more of a swale, one side of the watercourse a broad, flat bench above cut bank that was treeless except along the water's edge, the other side occasional cliffsides among steep slope forested with snow-dusted ponderosa pine and Doug fir.

The snow's depth increased proportionately to their rise in elevation, and slowed their going. The clouds finally opened as they rode, to drop a light but persistent fall of flurries. So far no wind had come up, but with the waning day, Holt could feel the temperature dropping steadily.

They were an hour upstream when he said, "This is as far as we go for now." He swung out of the saddle to forestall the argument he anticipated.

It didn't work. "There's daylight left," Sam protested.

"Yeah, and there's nothing I like better than making camp in pitch-dark." Holt faced her. "You ever done this before? Slept out when the temperature drops below zero, and a storm might bust wide open at any time?"

"No," she admitted.

"I have, and I'll tell you what could happen without fire, shelter, and enough clothing to beat the chill. First your lips turn blue and you shiver like an aspen in a gale. That's bad. Then you stop shivering—that's worse. The idea of dozing off is sweet as nectar, but if you do, you'll never wake up."

He'd reached her; she dismounted. "I'll gather wood," she said.

"You do that."

The exchange set the mood of the miserable evening. Although the snow fell no more vigorously, the cold deepened and there was no way the fire would be much succor once they fell asleep, assuming they were able to. After a supper of tinned beans, Holt jerry-rigged a shelter with their saddle blankets and his riata. It smelled bad and offered little relief from the chill, but at least kept them from being buried in the snowfall.

They turned in soon after; there was not much else to do. They wore every article of clothing they had packed, but sometime in the night Holt was awakened by noise.

Sam's teeth were chattering. In the subconsciousness of her sleep she must have felt her distress, because her hip was close against his.

Holt shook her. She moaned in a way that alarmed him, came awake sluggishly.

"Come closer," Holt said.

"What?" She was more fully conscious now.

"This has nothing to do with nothing," Holt said roughly,

feeling awkward, the more so over the short words they'd had around supper. "We need each other's warmth."

Holt pulled her into his arms, immensely embarrassed.

It got worse when she nestled against him. He could feel her warmth and every contour of her curves. "This is nice," she said. Her tone was stuporous, but gradually her body warmed against his and her shivering stopped.

"It's what we got to do," he said.

But she had fallen asleep again, this time more peacefully, and made no answer.

Holt awoke frequently, and when he did doze, dreams came. He was in blue uniform in one, marching endlessly through sucking mud in a driving rainstorm while gray-clad Rebs lurked just out of sight. In another he was back in prison with his old cellmate Billy Card, but in a cage so small that they were compelled to stand belly to belly, and bars were everywhere. Later he dreamt of erotic doings, the woman changing like a malevolent spirit from Sam to Cat Lacey to Charity Morgan.

Sam rolled over as Holt gave it up and disentangled himself from her to crawl from under the makeshift tarp. He built a driftwood fire using pine needles for starter; their natural oils made them excellent tinder. When it was going good enough, he added a log, fetched the coffeepot, and went to the horses.

They were picketed in the trees by the creek, where the ground was somewhat shielded and the snow less deep. During the night, the animals had managed to paw down to some dried grass and ferns. Holt led them to where the cut bank gave way to less steep slope. The roan was thirsty enough to step out on the three-foot shelf of ice fronting the open water; the bay, seeing it hold, followed suit.

When they drank their fill, Holt edged gingerly out to where they'd been. The ice covered a back-eddy pool, and when he knelt at its edge, he discovered it was a good half-foot thick. He shivered and filled the pot.

He took the horses back to camp, then piled on more

logs until the fire blazed heartily. From a saddlebag lying next to the tack, he dug a pint bottle of bourbon.

"A little early, wouldn't you say?" Sam emerged from her sleeping roll.

"Look." Holt turned the bottle upside down. The air bubble rose slowly through liquor that was gelid and syrupy. "Back-country thermometer," he explained.

"What's it read?"

Holt studied the viscid liquor. "Colder than a lawyer's handshake," he said.

He added grounds to the pot while Sam went down to the creek. Holt felt some concern: It should not have been so frigid with the cloud cover intact and promising snowfall. Much about this day was ominously portentous.

He sensed even greater extremes to come, extremes beyond which normal folks could not defend. A wolfer would be okay, likely, from habit and general toughness, but mortals like him and Sam were out of their element, in the literal sense. By the time she returned, coffee was boiling and Holt had come to a decision.

He put off the inevitable conflict while he fetched the skillet and a pound slab of bacon. It was frozen solid, of course, and no amount of sawing with his knife would do any effective slicing. By now there were embers in the fire; Holt piled some and set the bacon to cooking slowly while he found potatoes, hard as brown rocks. He poked them into the edge of the fire. By then the bacon was thawed enough so he was able to carve off pieces. If he left it to cook in a hunk, the inside would be raw as slaughterhouse beef.

The fire did little to warm him; Holt could swear that as dawn progressed, it perversely grew more frigid. Considering what he was about to tell Sam, his thoughts turned to the term "cold feet" and he smiled grimly. It was not that, but pure prudence, and she by God was going to be convinced. When he sliced the potatoes into the bacon fat, it sputtered and a few boiling flecks splatted the back of his hand. He could barely feel the burn of it.

Sam huddled close to the fire and sipped coffee. When Holt heaped dishes high with meat and potatoes, she said, "That's a hearty meal."

"Yeah, and you better clean your plate. A body needs fat and bulk in this weather."

Holt dug in; the food would not remain hot for long. "That's why we're turning back," he said.

Sam gave him the look he expected.

"In these conditions, our provisions won't last three days," Holt said, his mouth full.

"We could ration."

Holt pointed at her plate, already nearly empty. "In a half minute you've put away maybe a pound of grub."

"I'm always hungry at breakfast."

Holt did not intend to argue. "And you'll be hungry at dinner and supper as well, if we try stretching out what we've got."

He slurped down lukewarm coffee. "We can go on another day, but according to the map, we're still twenty miles from the headwaters of this drainage. We get caught in a deep freeze, we're a world away from help."

"We've come this far and we're doing all right. I say we take that other day. After that, I'll give no argument."

"We leave now," Holt insisted. "We regroup, we wait for the weather to mellow, and we provision heavy and take pack animals when it does." Holt finished the last of his breakfast. "And this is how it is going to happen," he declared.

Sam regarded him. "You're still worried about me."

"I'm worried for myself, goddamn it." It sounded overly harsh when it came out. "And you," he amended.

That was a mistake, though. "Then you're wrong," Sam said. She rose and went to work breaking camp and stowing gear.

Holt knew her well enough by now, and it was with resignation that he heard her say, twenty minutes later as they got horseback, "I'm riding upstream. You do what you want."

She was bluffing. "Good luck and so long," he said, and turned his horse in the direction of the prairie.

He walked the bay a hundred yards before the irritation of not hearing her behind him became unbearable and he gave up. He reined and wheeled, phrasing his capitulation in his mind, expecting to find her waiting angrily by the campsite.

Holt felt a sinking leaden feeling, and cursed himself for his arrogant "insights" into what she'd do.

Sam was nowhere in sight.

Chapter Ten

Portents weighed on Holt heavily as a shroud—his bad dreams, cautions to Sam about death from exposure, apprehensions voiced of hostile and proprietary wolfers, his insistence and Sam's rejection not an hour earlier....

In that brief span, Holt's feelings of foreboding had transmuted into incipient terror and rising desperation in his thus-far futile search for her.

He must take it slowly or risk ruining his horse. The footing was invisible under the deepening snow, and like him, the animal could hardly get enough energy into it through the scant feed it found. Did Sam understand this as well? In her anger and willfulness, there was no telling how fast she'd ridden, nor how far ahead she was.

Or up which path. The rising wind had obliterated any tracks.

In despair, Holt faced a divide in the creek. On the map the left course was labeled "Main Fork" and the right "North Fork," but both looked equally passable.

Holt hollered her name, the gale dashing the word back in his face.

Above and ahead the clouds were sooty black, and gravid with imminent storm. He could wait here, but what if she were pressing on, obstinate and unaware of the full nature of the peril? He must move, if only to avoid freezing stiff in the saddle. He bent his head and directed the horse up the Main Fork of Rock Creek.

Ten minutes later the black clouds exploded with snow.

For an eerie span of seconds the wind died completely,

but the snowfall was a deluge, as if the heavens were dumping the contents of a million feather beds all about him. Holt could barely see trees twenty feet distant.

Then the wind blasted, sending stinging particles into his face, and Holt could not see ahead at all.

Though he had heard tell of such phenomena, Holt had never been in a full whiteout blizzard before. It comprised instant claustrophobia close as a coffin, the natural world utterly obliterated.

His horse was also new to the experience. The bay whinnied in panic and made to flee this white hell. Holt tried and failed to jerk it to its senses; the horse quick-stepped back toward who knew what. Holt dismounted and pulled down hard on the reins.

The bay nickered madly, jerked free, and disappeared into the swirling miasma.

For a long moment Holt stood stock-still, straining his ears. He heard nothing but a rush like Pacific surf—indeed felt that he was drowning in the storm's density.

A blast of wind solid as a granite block knocked him over on his side.

He leaped immediately up—and wondered what was the purpose. He could not move on by foot, because he had no idea which direction he faced, and a wrong guess meant plunging over the cut bank into the icy creek. Yet if he stayed still he would freeze stony as a statue.

He whistled; the horse, if it heard, made no response. It might be within yards, or hundreds of yards.

He chose movement. After the one break in the gale, the blizzard blew with uncanny steadiness, the wind a constant buffeting that Holt kept to his right side. He prayed it was a westerly, meaning he was edging south and away from the creek.

One foot plunged downward as if the wind had whisked away the very surface on which he trod. Holt fell a second time and his ankle twisted and crackled.

He almost held his breath as he tried out the joint—it

moved, which meant it was not broken, though it hurt like the devil.

He could walk on it, though; he must. But first, he thought, he'd rest for a minute.

After a time he stopped shivering. Drowsily, he thought the wind might be abating. Soon the onslaught would cease. The bay would not have gone far, and he'd find it and Sam as well. She'd be okay, and the rightness of the world would return to him.

He'd need his strength. A brief nap seemed in order. As his eyes closed, some voice screamed at him to get up.

He made it shut up, and went away into darkness.

The Bible from which Holt's mother had taught him reading was illustrated, and as a child he'd been most impressed with the woodcut drawings of Satan. The demon was depicted with shaggy hair all over his body, cloven hooves, and from his form arose wavy lines labeled "sulfur."

Satan was standing over Holt now. The devil smiled to reveal fanglike yellowed teeth and slobbery lips buried deeply in the hairy visage.

"I ain't carrying no smelling salts," Satan said, "so I farted." The fiend laughed. "Looks like it did the trick."

Holt shuddered massively, no longer from dread, but from the cold that still racked his body. He was lying on a hard surface, and his clothing was soaking wet.

"You ought to be stripped down," the other presence said, "but I wasn't up to doing it myself."

Holt came further around, managed to sit up. His ankle was numb but no longer painful. He found himself on a plank floor surrounded by four walls of bare dirt, and above, a ceiling of wood. An iron stove glowed in the middle of the rude room.

His fingers were stiff when he fumbled at the buttons of his clothing, but he managed to get them off. When he was naked, he moved as close to the stove as he could without burning himself. His back, away from the heat, remained cold.

"Geeson."

Holt peered up, and the damned spirit became a man. "Is that your name?"

"I'll ask the questions," the man said. "Yes."

Besides the stove, Holt noted a rank sleeping pallet from which dried grass tufted, a jumble of tinned goods and other gear in one corner, and a few rude cooking implements hanging above a cut-dirt shelf.

"Others make fun," Geeson said. " 'Old man lives in a hole in the ground,' they needled. You from farm stock?"

"Ranch," Holt managed. He felt vulnerable without clothing, but life was reanimating within him, slowly but surely.

"You have a root cellar, for apples and 'taters and such?"

"Yeah."

"There it is. Reason for a root cellar is that underground the temperature don't change much, summer or winter. Now you see my point?"

The immediate point, Holt reckoned, was that he was face-to-face with a moron or a madman. What he'd mistaken for a hair-covered demon was a large man of middle to late years in a buffalo robe, and rather than cloven hooves, rubber boots. His hair hung over the robe's collar in stringy strands, and the small part of his face that was not bearded displayed a constellation of liver spots.

"I see your point," Holt said. "How'd you find me?"

"I'll ask the questions," Geeson said. "Dumb luck. Yours, not mine."

Atop the stove was a dented tin pot, from which a scent came that was not quite malodorous enough to dim Holt's hunger. Geeson drew a knife, a gesture moderately threatening until he used it to stir the pot's contents. "I got a romantic streak," he said. "I see the outdoors as a temple."

Geeson speared a chunk of something, gulped it down. "After the storm, I went for a walk. I like to observe nature—it's kind of a winter wonderland out there."

"I know." Holt turned to warm his back. "I was wondering if I was going to live." Within Geeson's dugout it was dim and quiet. "What time of day is it?"

"I'll ask the questions," Geeson said. "You were lying there covered in about a foot of snow. Appeared to be a grave, but with a certain human shape to it. I dusted you off and brought you in." Geeson gestured with the knife. " 'Why?' you're about to ask."

"You'll ask the questions," Holt said. "You got another robe I could maybe wear?"

Geeson gave him a look, but got up to dig something from a far corner of the room, tossed it at Holt. Holt fumbled the catch and the robe descended over him. It smelled like a varmint a horse had stomped and a coyote had fed on.

Holt wrapped it around him. Geeson showed his bad teeth again in a perceptive grin. "Wolfers are known for their stink. You don't have to wear it, you don't want."

"Thanks," Holt said, "for saving my life."

He felt a sudden jolt; in the surprise of finding himself resurrected, he'd forgotten Sam. "Did you see a woman?"

"Once or twice," Geeson said. "Last time was in a whorehouse in a town called Bozeman. She was buck naked, but she declined to go with me." Geeson dwelt fondly on the recollection. "Still, I cherish the memory."

"I was with a woman," Holt said, trying to get him back on track.

"Me, too, but longer ago than I can recall." Geeson impaled another chunk from the pot and chewed loudly. "Actually, I can recall. She looked to be a redhead, but when I got her stripped down—"

"Mr. Geeson," Holt interrupted.

Geeson came back from that time in the past. "You wolf, you lose yourself," he said.

Holt was growing increasingly frantic about Sam's whereabouts and condition, and feeling well enough to seek answers. At the same time, he knew he needed sustenance before he was in any fit shape for such pursuits.

"Can I have some of that stew?" he tried.

"I'll ask the questions." Geeson stirred the pot. "I suppose so."

He scooped up a mess of the concoction with a coffee cup. Holt took it, licked gravy from his fingers. It wasn't too bad. Geeson didn't offer a spoon, so Holt followed the mountain man's example and used his knife and fingers.

"You don't have the wolfer's look to you." Geeson peered at him. "What you got is the gunman's look. Why are you afoot in these parts?"

"My horse bolted during the storm. I got separated from my partner as well—the woman I was talking about."

Geeson wiped gravy from his beard. "This is neither the territory nor season for amateurs."

Holt was beginning to see that Geeson was more complex than first impression indicated. "If you had an extra animal I could borrow . . ."

"Don't have no animal at all," Geeson said. "I like to traipse." Geeson offered a greasy-lipped smile. "Looks like you got some traipsing before you your own self."

"It's got to be a dozen miles to Lobo."

"Give or take," Geeson said amiably.

"My horse probably hasn't wandered far," Holt said, half to himself.

"Good chance it's moving right now," Geeson contradicted. "With someone on its back. Wolfers sort of believe in finders-keepers—except for others' pelts, of course."

Holt finished the stew. "I'd call that thievery."

"Call it what you'd like," Geeson said. "You want some more stew?"

Holt gave him the cup. "Thanks."

If Sam made it through the storm, she was still at the mercy of any stranger she ran into. Holt felt depressed and guilty; letting her get out of his sight was the last in a string of stupid decisions, beginning with coming up here without sufficient preparation in the first place.

"I've got to find her."

Geeson shrugged. "There ain't but three hours of daylight left. Also, I'd want dry clothes, but maybe that's just me."

Geeson went to the corner of the dugout where the gear was jumbled, returned with a mallet, nails, and a length of rope. Holt stood for the first time, without great difficulty. The food and the warmth of the fire had brought his body temperature back up to normal. He helped Geeson rig the rope above the stove—the ceiling was barely two inches higher than his head—and hung his sodden duds.

Geeson gave him the second cup of stew. It really wasn't that bad at all, chunks of meat in flour gravy with lots of salt. "Bear?"

"Wolf," Geeson said. "Waste not, want not." When Holt was not quick enough to hide a wince of distaste, Geeson looked wounded. "Chinamen eat dogs, which is a damned heathen sight worse," he said defensively.

"It's good," Holt assured him.

"I'll ask the questions," Geeson said, "and you haven't answered one of them. Who are you looking for?"

Holt was startled, wondered if he'd talked in his sleep.

"We already figured out you ain't a wolfer. No one in his right mind would come up here after game when there's plenty on the prairie. And you sure as hell ain't out to see the sights." Geeson pointed at the sleeping pallet, atop which his belt and his Colt lay; Holt had been too disoriented to notice it missing when he'd come around, another minor stupidity.

"You're carrying a gunhand's kind of weapon," Geeson continued his deductions. "That just about leaves out any possibility except that you're after someone. Who?"

"I'd just as soon not say," Holt tried.

"I ask the questions," Geeson said, "and that's not a polite answer."

Or a smart one, either; Geeson was already suspicious.

"Here is why I wolf," he said. "I'm not much fond of people, on account of they are always trying to lead each other around by their short hairs. Don't try such with me."

This was push come to shove. Holt drew a deep breath. "I think you are full of bull."

When Geeson stood, he had to bend his neck to keep from bumping the ceiling. Irrelevantly, Holt thought: When he'd made this place, why hadn't he dug down a half-foot deeper? Geeson growled, which quickly brought Holt back to the matter at hand.

"What sort of crack is that?" Geeson balled his fists, looking quite as demonic as Holt in his half-frozen state had first perceived him.

"Settle down," Holt said. "I only meant that I don't think you hate folks. I think you are enjoying my company."

"Not for much longer," Geeson said. "You talk truth, or I'll throw your buck-naked ass into the snow and slam the hatch behind you. I got a healthy curiosity."

If he didn't give Geeson something, Holt reasoned, the old wolfer was sure to tell Gutt about him anyway. His best chance was that Geeson hadn't completely abandoned civilized decency and judgment.

"Gutt committed a crime that got blamed on me," Holt said. "I need him to clear me."

"A killing crime?"

"That's right."

Geeson knitted his brow as if working out equations. "Why ain't you in stir?"

Holt was in too deep now. He explained, and because Geeson was sure to ask, admitted there was a price on his head. He left Sam out of that part of the story.

Geeson was silent for some time. "I got to believe you, 'cause you don't strike me as so stupid you'd make up something that'd put your head in the noose." He looked at Holt as if measuring him for the rope himself. "Reckon you are worth a hell of a lot more than a pile of wolf pelts."

"You can help me save *my* pelt."

Geeson might not have heard. He cocked his head toward his gear, on which was propped a Remington 306. "All I got to do is shoot you."

"You plan to?"

"I'm pondering on it." Geeson rose, and Holt felt alarm.

"I guess not," Geeson said after a bit. "Never have, don't want to start at my age."

"Huh?"

"I'll ask the questions," Geeson said automatically, but his mind was elsewhere. "Never had to. I'm too big and scary."

"I'll warrant," Holt muttered.

Geeson wasn't paying him any mind. "You're right: I've got to believe that you are the victim of a miscarriage of justice." He shook his shaggy head. "Too bad. I sort of like Gutt."

Holt saw a glimmer of optimism. "So he is in these parts?"

"We've played a hand of pinochle now and then," Geeson said. "He craved companionship."

"And he put me in a hell of a pickle," Holt said, trying to bring the discussion back to the topic on his mind.

"He's up there somewhere," Geeson said, "but that is all you will get from me."

"What'll he get from you? You plan to inform on me?"

"Another question. Watch yourself." Geeson considered. "I suppose that's something you'll have to worry about."

Wonderful, Holt thought. Just ducky.

"Lend me some clothes," Holt said.

"Ain't got but what I'm wearing."

Holt pondered. "You know these parts."

"Better'n my own mother." Geeson considered the metaphor. "Lots better," he decided.

"I'll pay you a hundred dollars to help me find my partner."

"Okay," Geeson said readily. "In which of your pockets will I find such geetus?"

"I'm good for it."

Geeson used a finger to scrape the last of the gravy from the stew pot, oblivious to the heat. "That's a gamble I won't take. Looks like you are on your own."

Holt started to say something, but Geeson raised a finger

to silence him. "But here is some advice. You ain't going anywhere today, not anywhere you can expect to reach. Spend the night, gather your strength, and on the morrow you are on your own. That is far as I can take it."

The thought of a claustrophobic stay in this hole was abysmal, but the alternative, afoot in the dark and fumbling about, went beyond abysmal to insane.

"Help yourself to the amenities," Geeson said. "Me, I'm turning in for a nap." He went to the pallet, pushed Holt's gun aside as if it were a sack of nails, and flopped down.

Holt stared as Geeson began to snore. He felt like an animal in a pit trap, as if the dugout were a hundred miles deep and the weight of the entire planet oppressed him.

Chapter Eleven

Sam willed herself to set aside emotion in favor of rational thought. Holt was horseless, and beyond her ability to help. The only one of them she could save was herself, and that meant riding out alone—and immediately.

She checked the rope that ran from the back strap of her saddlebags to the halter of Holt's bay, sighed heavily, and started downtrail, cursing vehemently, as she had been for most of the last several hours.

She'd gone a half mile up from the fork before realizing she'd chosen the wrong branch of Rock Creek, all the time cursing Holt's stubbornness in lieu of acknowledging her own. By then she saw that the valley narrowed to cliff-walled canyon on both sides, enclosing roiling rapids that would not freeze even in this cold. While she could see bench land no more than fifty feet upstream, only a mountain goat could reach it. In the mental flip of a coin that had determined her pick at the forks, she'd come up tails.

The poor bet likely saved her hide.

Twice when she was growing up in Boston, hurricanes had come up the Atlantic coast to besiege the city. From her parents' brick house near the top of Beacon Hill, she gazed out the window at the Common with a child's fascination at nature's power, while winds toppled massive-trunked trees to expose huge circles of roots that looked like witches' hair, and deluging rain dug runnels in the park's sloping manicured lawns.

Compared to the whiteout blizzard, a hurricane was a summer shower.

The only forewarning was a nervous nicker from her roan. Moments later it was snowing sideways.

Her good fortune was that the storm was roaring from the west, and the niche where she was stopped from advancing upstream was alee. She got herself and the horse into it, talking in a low meaningless monotone to gentle the animal. Providentially, the roan calmed, seemed willing to wait it out.

Not that either had any choice.

She wrapped herself in the robe and pulled her neckerchief up over her nose and lips, so only her eyes were exposed. She was neither hungry nor thirsty, but chewed on jerked beef and drank from the canteen that hung by a lanyard under her shirt, so it would not freeze. Holt had showed her that trick when they broke camp that morning.

Holt was much on her mind as she huddled, feeling as if she were a hundred leagues down in a sea of white.

She had no sense of time, knew only that the tempest ended as abruptly as its onset. The wind fairly screeched to a stop, like a steam engine braking frantically for a wagon high-centered on the tracks. Snow no longer fell at all, and she could see the canyon and the creeks and the sky. In the time it took to gather herself, repack the blankets, and adjust the jumble in her saddlebags caused when she'd dug out the jerky, holes of wan blue began to break through the cloud cover. When she checked her watch, she was surprised to see that she had been holed up less than an hour.

She felt light-headed with relief and good cheer as she started back toward the forks. Of course Holt had weathered the onslaught, and likely better than she; he knew the ways of this sort of country. He'd sheltered in some cave or dugout, rolling cigarettes and admiring nature's fury.

He'd worry about her, certainly, but that was too bad. She felt proud; she was looking forward to telling him how well she'd done, how she'd remembered all the survival lore he'd imparted to her.

Pigheaded as he was, there was not one chance in a million that he truly would ride down from this country without her. He was at the forks, waiting for her to appear. She could see the parting of the waters a hundred yards ahead. Giddily, she recalled their night together. . . .

She spotted his horse and her heart jumped. The bay stood by the bank, below where the two streams tumbled together, drinking at the edge of an open pool. She called Holt's name as she rode up to it.

The bay looked at her curiously and went back to drinking. No other response greeted her repeated and increasingly frantic hollers.

Logic plucked at her sleeve. It was demanding, not to be denied, and ever more irksome as the next few hours passed. It told her that Holt could not possibly have pressed on during the storm, but must have stopped and taken shelter. It said that he could not have lost his horse except sometime between the storm's beginning and end, which in turn meant he could not have moved far. It asked why he would move in any case, when he was so close to the fork and needed only to wait for her and the use of her horse to find his own.

There was one question only to which logic did not offer answer: How could he have disappeared from the earth's face?

She rode a couple miles up the Main Fork and uncovered not the slightest sign of him, living or dead. Now she turned downstream from the branch, with the same dismal result.

She scanned the slopes for the shelter she'd imagined; none existed. The only further explanation she could think of was chilling, figuratively and literally: in the whiteout, he'd stumbled into the creek.

She denied that awful thought as she sat her horse where she'd finished her search, but much as she dreaded the notion, she had to face the truth that he was gone.

In that case, he'd want her to see to herself.

If she left his horse, at best it would be taken by some wolfer, at worst it would die of exposure. Either fate was a distinct possibility for her as well. In the few hours of daylight left, she could make it down to prairie, from where the remaining ride to Morgan's in the dark was far less risky.

The bay whinnied as she remounted, as if it knew something she didn't. Sam put the mountaintops and the oncoming twilight to her back and started away from there.

The going was significantly tougher than she'd expected, and she made poor time. Despite its brevity, the blizzard's enormous power had wrought profound changes, even breaking up the ice on stretches of the creek. It must have dumped the better part of a foot of snow, distributed by the gale in random and capricious ways. In some places the ground was scoured clear, and she stopped each time the horses wanted to take advantage and feed. In other places, in the wind shadow of trees or rocks or for no apparent reason, snow was drifted as deep as the horses' bellies, and they plunged and snorted in great steamy gasps as they breasted it.

Darkness caught her still well within the creek valley, though the clouds had mostly swept on and there was sufficient starlight to illuminate her way. But with clearing came plunging temperature, and even draped with both of her blankets over her robe, she was cold. To add to the tenuousness of her situation, she was growing weary, for this had been a day of exertions.

An hour later she passed the painted rocks that indicated the gate of the valley was not far ahead. She was adjusting the blankets when she saw the two men riding upstream.

The narrowness of the valley here where it was bound by the painted-rock walls offered no hiding place. For a moment she considered retreating, before setting the notion aside as suicidal; she'd never survive another night, especially not alone.

She drew her Colt and hid it under the blankets' folds, rode on as if she had as much right to be in these precincts as anyone. She'd say howdy and move on past.

That was not to be. Soon as they made her out, the men

set their horses side by side and somewhat apart, effectively blocking the trail. "Who's that?" one called.

Sam rode up and said, "Nice evening, if a tad cold."

"What the hell?" The one on the right was burly, and his face, where it was visible before the bandanna wrapped over his ears, was bearded.

The other gaped at her through dark, deep-socketed eyes. Like his partner, he wore a buffalo robe, but within its swathing he must have been a slight being; his head was small and peeked out incongruously from the volume of the coat, like a turtle's from its shell.

"Ain't this the damnedest," the big one said. "Just t'other day I was thinking about women."

"Me, too, Farley." The little one sounded a bit dim, as if perhaps his little apple head was too small to house much brain.

"I'll be moving on," Sam said.

Farley looked around elaborately. Behind the men were tethered two mules loaded down with supplies. "Not just yet," Farley said.

Sam gestured at the pack animals. "You been down to see Quint."

"So what?"

Sam pushed the bluff. "He mentioned me, likely."

"No."

"I'm under his protection," Sam said. "He was supposed to put the word out." She assayed a smile. "I am writing about wolfers for a magazine called *Harper's*." This worked on occasion; ruffians might back off from journalists, as from a lawman, or they might like the idea of getting their names in an article. "I expect you've heard of it."

"He can't read," the applehead said. "Me neither."

"Shut up, Moon." Farley pondered on matters. "You know Quint?"

"I said I did. It wouldn't go well for someone who mistreated me." The cold was penetrating her blankets, and she worked on not shivering, from the chill and the situation.

"How'd he know who done it?" Farley said, smiling shrewdly.

"Done what?" Moon asked.

"What we reckon to do." The smile broadened. "See, what I'm thinking, we take her up with us, keep her around awhile. When we got our fill, we . . . well, just let's say it's a long ways to first thaw."

"I don't get it, Farley," Moon said.

Farley was still working out his plan. "Also, we can always use extra horses." He gestured at Holt's bay. "Where'd you steal 'em?"

The scene, to Sam, had progressed beyond peril to what, if it hadn't been so dire, would be something like farce. She took the Colt out from under the blanket and said, "Time for you both to give up on your nasty ideas."

"You plan on shooting us if we don't?" Farley was amused.

"That's right." Sam watched both men's hands for any quick move. "You mean to steal my horses, abduct me, and brutalize—"

"What's brutalize?"

"Shut up, Moon," Farley said again.

"—and you expect I won't use this if I have to?" Sam finished.

"You won't."

Sam fired, missing by a close enough margin to get his thoughtful attention.

Farley spit into the snow, stared up at the stars and shook his head. "Nope," he decided. "I bet you can't do it."

He walked his horse toward her.

Sam said, "You lose," and shot him in the thigh.

Moon yelped. Farley winced, pulled his horse up and reached under his robe. Sam fired again, cutting a furrow through the coat's fringe without striking flesh. Farley's hand came out, slowly and empty.

"Ride on," Sam said. "You'll be in my sights until you're out of range."

Moon licked his lips. "Guess we're going, huh, Farley?"

Farley glared blackly at Sam. "I ain't gonna die, not from some puny flesh wound. I ain't gonna forget neither." He spurred his horse cruelly enough to make the animal whinny, rode too closely by her. "When I say *Hasta luego*, you can depend on the *luego* part. You and me aren't done."

She could smell his rank breath. "I'll do you," Farley said, "down in the dirt where you and every other woman belong, and afterward—" He grinned horribly. "—afterward'll come the real fun."

Sam watched them until they disappeared into the night, and waited fifteen minutes more, giving in now to the urge to shudder, at what might have been and what might still come. As the time passed, she thought about what further harm might develop from this encounter: talk of a woman up this drainage, talk that might reach Gutt, obvious enough when deciphered to allow him to put one and one together and come up with her and Holt.

But then, Holt was no longer a problem, as Gutt would also come to learn.

She wallowed in that ugly thought until she was sure they weren't planning to backtrack, then turned and continued on out of the valley, stopping every hundred yards or so to check behind anyway.

Beyond the mouth of the drainage she made faster progress, taking the trail by which they'd gone in and giving Lobo a mile's worth of berth. But by the time she was abreast of the town, its squat buildings just visible to the south in the starshine, she knew that plans had to be revised. The odds of making Morgan's in one piece had grown exceedingly long.

The clue was when her horse half bucked and she barely managed to catch the reins and keep her seat. She'd fallen asleep in the saddle.

The animal sensed her momentary absence of control, and cranky with hunger and thirst, tried to bolt. She got it gentled, but the experience was sobering. A number of things, none good, could happen if she got unhorsed. But making a camp, she decided, was out of the question. She didn't have the skills or experience to do it on her own, and it would leave her exposed to peril, natural and human.

She studied the town again, sighed deeply, and without further internal debate rode in that direction.

If not for the starlight, Lobo would have been dark as a crypt. No window was lit and no person was abroad; the overall effect was so spectral it might have been a literal ghost town.

She hitched the two horses in front of the saloon and climbed down. Behind the bat-wing doors permanent shutters were bolted. Sam pounded on them with a balled fist. They bent and creaked, the noise carrying on the night air. In the desolate street behind her, the horses pawed and tossed their heads, as if remonstrating at her foolishness.

The shutters swung open. Sam recoiled, expecting to face an aggressive Quint. She reached for her Colt, but then forebore. No gun when you're petitioning for room at the inn, she thought.

She was confabulating, and must get in out of the cold before too much time passed. She steadied herself with a hand on the doorjamb to avoid falling on her face.

Emma Franks gave her a long evaluating look before stepping aside. Sam entered past her. Quint stood behind the bar, holding a lit match to the wick of an oil lamp. He trimmed it, and the light glinted off his steel jaw. "Look what the cat drug in," he observed.

Sam slumped into the nearest chair. She was not overly worried about Quint now; she'd already figured out that Emma kept him on a short leash, although Sam didn't know how she managed it.

Emma sat opposite her, stared some more. After a time she said to Quint, but looking at Sam, "Bring her a drink."

The lamp provided minimal illumination, which served to emphasize the shadowy sparseness of the room. At least it was warm; the stove still glowed faintly with the evening's fire. Quint brought over a quarter tumbler of whiskey.

"I'll need to see to my horses," Sam said.

"Horses," Emma echoed thoughtfully. "Yours and your man's?"

Sam nodded.

"Where is he?" Quint said.

"You're too tuckered," Emma said to Sam, as if Quint had not spoken. "Take care of 'em, Quint."

He did not argue, but on the way out he said, "Hold off on the palaver until I get back."

Sam left the glass where it was; a few sips and she was a sure thing to pass out face first on the table. Emma went on staring rigidly, hardly blinked.

"I'd take it kindly if I could stay the night," Sam said. "I'll sleep on the floor."

For all the response she got, she might have been speaking to a telegraph post.

Quint returned by and by, and after fetching himself a drink, went to stand by the stove's warmth. "You bushwhack your pard and steal his horse and outfit?" He laughed.

"She wants to sleep on the floor," Emma said, as if this provided some significant insight into Sam.

"Where is he?" Quint said for the second time.

This conversation, meandering here, veering sharply there, was making Sam dizzy. Absently she sipped at the whiskey, which increased her vertigo. "We got separated."

"That's evident," Emma snapped. "Now you listen up: the barn where your horses are is locked. So's every other building in town. With the citizens we got, you watch your property close."

Only her mouth moved as she spoke. "So think about what would happen if I kicked you out of here, which I will, you don't tell what happened."

Sam hesitated. Emma sprang from her chair, quick as a snake. She was around the table before Sam could fully rise, and Emma jerked her the rest of the way up with one hand, slapped her face with the other, as Sam had seen her strike Quint.

"You like to slap people," Sam said.

Emma was surprisingly strong, and barely paid attention when Sam tried to pull free. Emma marched her toward the door, murmured nastily, "I guess this is good night."

"I'll talk," Sam said.

Emma half dragged her back to the table, dumped her in the chair, took her own place. From behind the bar where he was pouring another drink, Quint looked amused, as if this byplay was lighting up an otherwise boring night. "What are you gawking at?" Emma snapped.

Sam told how she had lost Holt. When she finished, Quint said, "We got the wind but not the snow. I could see it up there, though, the whole front covered in storm thick as chop suey. I'm thinking of my men, o' course, but them boys is hard to kill. You could drop one down a two-hundred-foot shaft, and he'd land on his feet and claw his way out."

He poured another drink and added, "Yours is dead, though."

"We heard one story," Emma said. "Let's hear the other. No nonsense about rustlers and Indians and Morgan—none of that's why you came here, you and him, that's clear as crystal spring water and something I already figured out last time we chatted. Now I'll have the true reason."

Sam took another drink and the liquor made her gag. A mouthful of it came back up, bile-bitter and nauseating. She staggered to the bar, spewed it into a spittoon. That made her gag again, but there was nothing left to come up.

When she turned, Emma stood before her, hands on hips. "You'll change your mind by and by," she said.

Sam caught a glimpse of movement at her back, spun around. Quint stood spread-legged, a bung starter raised in both hands.

Sam danced away and the blow grazed her hat brim, knocking it off but losing power as it glanced off her shoulder. She pulled her gun, saw too late Emma on her flank.

Fingers held stiff, Emma brought the edge of her bony hand down on Sam's wrist. The revolver dropped away, clattered on the plank floor. Emma swung at her face. Exhaustion and nausea robbed Sam of coordination, and though the punch missed her nose by an inch, in evading it, she fell backward.

Emma was upon her, pinning her down with uncanny strength. The woman grabbed two handfuls of Sam's hair, jerked her head up. Sam's right hand wasn't working as it should, and she could not form a fist. She used her left to punch Emma in the stomach, hard as she could. Emma grunted fetid breath and momentarily released her. Sam hit her again, in the breastbone.

Emma rolled away, but at the same time grasped both of Sam's forearms. She pulled Sam to her feet, twirled her around as if they were engaged in some macabre dance, slammed her hard against the bar.

In the lamplight, Sam saw the shadow of Quint's form, the bung starter raised up again. She tried to move, but Emma's grip was entire.

Sam's head exploded into a flash of luminescence, snuffed immediately by all-consuming blackness.

Chapter Twelve

With his skinning knife Geeson sawed fatty meat from what looked like a dog's haunch. "I store it up on the roof next to the stovepipe, the idea being to keep it from getting either froze or spoilt. Tricky business." He separated a slab and examined it with a critical eye. "This side took a little heat and it's turned a mite green," he decided, "but I've et greener."

Holt finished pulling on the last of his clothing; it was stiff and smelled like everything else in the dugout, but at least was dry. He'd slept fitfully on the dirt under the buffalo robe, and felt gritty and even more out of sorts than on most mornings.

"You got coffee?" he asked.

"I'll ask the questions." Geeson found a tin container. "I got chickory."

"I got tobacco," Holt said. "We can work something out."

He made cigarettes while Geeson boiled the brew and grilled the wolf meat in a filthy skillet. They ate and then smoked in silence, the first cigarette of the day providing Holt with its usual laxative effect. It took both of them to raise the trapdoor in the ceiling against the weight of the snow, a good deal of which cascaded down inside Holt's collar.

When he boosted himself out, the beauty of the day struck him square in the gut.

The sun had not risen above the ridgetop, but its rays glittered off the highest part of the slopes, turning them to fields of white diamonds. Above, the sky was pure blue, and the air calm as a padre in the confessional. Not a branch moved on the trees by the creek, which ran only a few yards from Geeson's dugout. The temperature had risen during the night, and the rage of the previous day's blizzard was just a memory.

Pretty as it was, it could not drive fears for Sam from Holt's mind. He was thinking of her as he came out of the bushes, and face-to-face with the wolf.

Holt stumbled back. The animal was ten feet distant and showing no gesture of aggression. It lay doglike but alert in the snow, paws stretched in front of it, staring at Holt calmly. Its gray fur was thick and soft, marked by a collar of dark black. It bent its head to lick ice from between its toes, and after that decided Holt was no threat. It got to its feet and turned away.

Holt sighed, drew his Colt and shot the animal through the temple.

It flopped over and lay instantly still, without even a last twitch of life. That should have made it easier; instead it made Holt painfully aware, in the aftermath of the act, of the time he'd been shot himself by a creature to whom he offered no threat.

Geeson nudged at the dead wolf with the toe of his boot. "Fine pelt." He seemed to sense Holt's ambivalence. "Majestic, ain't they?"

"How's that?"

Geeson stuffed what remained of the breakfast into a canvas sack. "It was hard for you to shoot." It wasn't a question.

They stood aside the dugout's trapdoor. "I got a long walk ahead of me," Holt said.

"Life is a long walk," Geeson said, "but a man does what he must." Geeson regarded the dead wolf. "I wish you luck, and I say that sincerely."

Steam rose from the blood around the animal's head.

Geeson had something on his mind, and Holt suspicioned he was about to hear what it was.

"Pelt like that is worth six bucks, down to Fort Benton next spring," Geeson said. "You done me a good turn, even though it went against your nature."

"Wanted to repay your hospitality." Holt was itchy to get moving.

"So I'll go against my nature in return. This wolf you give me puts me in a kindly frame of mind."

"Meaning . . . ?"

Geeson dropped to one knee and his knife flashed in the morning brightness. The wolf's guts spilled and steamed on the snow. "Maybe we'll palaver again sometime," Geeson said.

Holt watched him skin one haunch and sever the meat from the joint.

"Meanwhile," Geeson said, prepossessed by his labors, "you'd best be on your way." Geeson shot him a shallow smile. "Like you mentioned, you got a long walk ahead of you."

Holt's ankle had healed up overnight enough so it supported him and he could walk without limping, though it still hurt. In other circumstances the pain would have been minor, but with more than a dozen miles to go, it was bothersome.

Nothing for that, he thought, and he'd seen worse days for travel. The sunshine reached the valley floor and the day became almost balmly. Frequent enough breaks in the creek ice provided drinking water, and besides the breakfast leftovers, the rucksack contained sufficient wolf jerky for the voyage. Keeping a steady pace, he'd be out of the mountains by not long after midday, he reckoned. There he might run into someone who could give him a lift, or take word to Morgan.

Or even Sam, come looking for him . . .

This he wanted desperately to believe, not so much for his own succor, but as indication she was alive and well.

But when he passed the forks, fifteen minutes after leaving Geeson, his hopes grew dimmer. He'd half expected—foolishly, he thought now—that she'd be waiting there.

She wasn't. That was the way of it, and he'd have to accept it. If she had survived the blizzard, she was okay now; if not ... He continued downstream, occasionally struggling through drifted snow.

Before he'd whittled more than a single mile off those to be covered, he heard the chuff of a horse. He jerked up his head, saw two riders trailing pack animals. Maybe his ticket out, he thought with foolish optimism.

As he got a closer look, that chance seemed less likely. These were wolfers, although the one with the odd too-small head seemed puny for the part. He said, in a thin alto voice, " 'Nother stranger, Farley."

"No shit, you chowder-wit," Farley snarled, with irritation out of proportion to the other's comment.

Holt assayed a neutral howdy. The little hombre said howdy back. Farley snapped, "Shut up, Moon," and to Holt: "Who are you, and what are you doing in my valley?"

"Leaving," Holt said. "I lost my horse in a storm while I was visiting a pal. Maybe you know him—ornery cuss name of Geeson."

"I know him, and the hell with him." Farley's horse sidestepped and Farley winced. "What if I said you were a liar?"

Holt smiled, friendly as he could manage. "I'd be offended," he said, "but I'd likely get over it."

Farley's robe was open, and a neckerchief was tied around his left thigh. A circle of mostly dry blood the size of a twenty-dollar gold piece spotted it where it covered the meaty part of his upper leg, and likely explained his sour demeanor.

"Maybe you mean to horn in on my wolfing territory," Farley said, "or maybe you are just general trouble."

Some glimmer of notion flashed in Moon's otherwise

dull gaze. "That girl with the two horses," he said. "I bet—"

Farley turned on him. "I told you once to shut up. Third time I won't be telling."

"You've seen a woman?" Holt felt hope warm as the sun's rays.

"Last night," Moon said.

Farley punched him in the side of the head, toppling him from the saddle. Moon landed on his face.

"She's the bitch that shot me," Farley said. "She yours?"

Holt shrugged noncommittally.

"I catch up with her," Farley said darkly, "you're going to be riding alone."

Holt had done a good job so far in not rising to any bait, and stuck to the tactic. "Speaking of riding," he said, "I need an animal. I'll make it worth your while."

"In a pig's valise," Farley snapped.

"I'll be moving along, then," Holt said.

Moon stirred.

"You don't strike me as much of a man," Farley said. "You can't hold on to your horse nor your woman, and you got a glib way of ducking a fight."

"You want a fight, that's up to you."

Moon managed to sit up. Farley regarded him absently, as if trying to recall who he was. "Good idea." Farley dismounted. "I been angry anyway since your girl shot me, and looking for some way to work it off."

Holt was hoping the leg wouldn't hold up, but it seemed to serve, although Farley limped and grimaced with each step. If it wasn't broken, at least a bone chip was floating around and digging in.

Off the horse, Farley was huge, and getting bigger with each approaching step. When he was a yard away, Holt said, "Wait up. There's something first."

"What?" Farley said.

"This."

Holt raised his boot and stomped it down on Farley's thigh. The kick was awkward and Holt stumbled, but stayed on his feet. Farley yowled and went down, grabbed his leg, rolled in the snow. That was plenty enough time for Holt to get his gun out.

"You busted it for true," Farley moaned.

"No I didn't. Stand up."

Farley did. The leg wasn't broken after all.

"I won't take a man's horse, but I'm going to have to borrow one of those mules," Holt said. "Unload it. You can come back for your gear later, and the mule will be at Quint's barn by tomorrow."

"You ain't taking nothing of mine."

"Afraid I am."

A gun went off behind Farley. He winced again. Moon still sat in the snow, but now he was holding a horse pistol that looked huge in his almost dainty hand. " 'Fraid you're not," Moon said.

Holt hesitated.

"Put it away," Moon said. "You ain't gonna use it, but I'll shoot and never think about it again. Us wolfers is a vicious lot."

For a simpleton, he could figure a thing or two. Holt did as he was told. About the only lucky break at this point was that Farley was hurting too bad to press any notions of fistfighting. That was good; with even odds, Holt had no doubt Farley would pound the stuffing out of him.

Farley climbed painfully back into the saddle. Moon followed suit, keeping Holt covered.

"We'll be spreading the word among the wolfers," Farley said, "and you decide on another visit to our territory, a dozen'll be ready to shoot first and take names second."

Riding past, Farley reined for a moment to spit with perfect accuracy, the globule landing an inch in front of Holt's boot toe. "Watch your back, pilgrim," he said.

Sam came awake but could not move, lay paralyzed for maybe three seconds. This happened to her now and then, and was invariably accompanied by a momentary blank on where she was.

Her body unfroze and she sat up, swinging her legs over the side of the thin mattress. She was fully clothed, although her robe had been removed and lay hunched in the corner like a sleeping animal. She was cold, but felt better once she got it on.

She was in a single-room cabin with one window, no bigger than her neckerchief, that looked out on another building that might have been the barn. Outside it was full daylight.

Besides the pallet on which she'd slept, the room contained only a table covered in oilcloth on which sat a pitcher of water and a chamber pot. She drank from the former and used the latter. Squatting brought a vicious jolt of pain to her head, and memory of being slugged the night before. She went to the door, and when she pushed at it, her wrist spasmed as well. The fingers worked now, at least, so no bones were broken, but Emma's blow must have pinched a nerve. With her left hand Sam shoved harder at the door, which gave a fraction of an inch. A padlock rattled on the other side.

She calmed herself. Eventually Quint—or Emma—would come, which had its up- and downsides, mostly devolving from what might happen after that.

Whatever time she had in the meanwhile, she decided, ought to be devoted to coming up with a story. As a magazine writer, she'd been under deadline before, but in this case, she felt she could safely assume, failing to meet it would have somewhat more dire results than merely an editor's wrath.

Chapter Thirteen

Factors conspired to prove optimistic Holt's estimate of his travel time. Stomping Farley did his ankle little good, and in boots he wasn't shod for walking in any case. The fine weather, while definitely superior to a repeat of the blizzard, had its disadvantages, the sun's rays setting up the snow from powder to gumbo that in places was shin-deep, and drawing sweat under the heavy robe that nonetheless turned chill when he tried removing it.

The sun dipped below the mountains to his back before he finally reached the prairie at the mouth of Rock Creek, with full dark in the near future. In any case, he doubted he could go much farther. His feet were woefully sore, enough so he dare not remove his boots to examine what felt like a wealth of blisters. If he did, his dogs would swell up and he'd never get reshod.

A night in the open, while not a particularly pleasant prospect, was his likely fate, and here was a better place than on the open range. The creek provided water, some shelter among the brush, and fuel; the branches of driftwood tossed to the bank during spring runoff were dry under their snow cover.

Among the cottonwood snags, Holt found a seat-sized flat rock. He dusted off the snow and wrestled it against a tree trunk, then gathered wood into a pile a couple feet from the rock. With his knife he split some of the smaller pieces into kindling, and managed to coax it to life on his fifth match. While the fire grew to robustness, he wiped the last of the snow from his makeshift chair and waited for any meltings to dry. By the time he settled down to sup on jerky, he was satisfied that he'd survive the night, or at least weather its elements, and in moderate comfort.

He smoked after the cold meal, then wrapped his arms around his knees and gazed at the flames, thinking the situation out under the serenity of the starry night.

If the object of their expedition into the mountains was to find Gutt, it had not been a total failure. This Farley character would talk, as men in isolated parts always did, and Gutt would put names to the man and woman he and Moon had run into. Would Gutt then run or come after them? No way to be sure, but Holt could not help but recall Gutt's promise at their meeting in Utah: to kill him if he approached again.

He thought of the odd duck Geeson, and the Morgans, the rancher and his brother Prospect and his strange daughter Charity, the allegations of Indian rustling, Quint and Gutt and Emma.

And Sam, lying close to him two nights previous, her softness and her warmth through all the clothing they both wore . . .

A billow of increasingly erotic thoughts rose, and on its crest Holt dozed.

Awkwardly slumped on the rock, he would have slept fitfully anyway, but he'd long ago learned the trick of willing himself to awake after a set period. The fire had to be fed hourly.

The third time he roused himself, he was not alone.

The bulk of a figure crouched on the other side of the flame, tending to Holt's chore for him. "Saw your setup. It looked inviting." The figure rose. "Didn't mean to wake you."

That seemed a mild enough introduction, and besides, if this man meant mischief, Holt thought, it would have already occurred while he was in dreamland. The fire fed on the fresh fuel and flared up, so Holt made him out more clearly. He had very dark hair that descended in two oiled braids over a buckskin jacket, and wore matching pants and moccasins of soft leather. First glance revealed no evident armament, although there was room for some under the blanket draped over his shoulders.

"I've seen you." Holt shook cobwebs from his half-asleep brain, tried to place the man. "With Charity Morgan, while we were gathering cows."

"Fool's Eagle," the man said.

From the creek came a noise, and Holt smelled horse fart.

"My name," the Indian explained.

Holt nodded. "I'm—"

"I know who you are," Fool's Eagle said.

Holt wouldn't have minded knowing what Charity had to do with this fellow, and exactly how much he did know. He settled on asking, "Blackfeet?"

Fool's Eagle had a dusky handsome face, which creased now into a sardonic smile. "And then, seeing as how you work for Morgan," he said, "you'll want to talk rustling." He poked a stick into the fire, watching its end glow and then burst into flame. Fool's Eagle shook his head. "Ask are my people stealing his cows."

"Are you ... I mean, they?"

This time the Indian laughed. "Yes and no. I'll show you."

"When?"

Fool's Eagle made a gesture, as if that were a stupid question at this time of night. "You didn't find him," he said.

"Find who?"

"The big man, calls himself Gutt."

This Indian certainly seemed up on current events—mostly his, Holt thought. "How do you come by all this information?"

Fool's Eagle shrugged. "I move around and I keep my eyes and ears open. Quint'll talk to me."

"I thought he hated Indians like a cat hates a bath."

"Worse," Fool's Eagle said, "if you believe all he spouts.

But some of it's an act, and anyway he'll take our money or trade goods. I'm the one deals with him."

"Why you?"

Fool's Eagle stared into the fire and smiled humorlessly at some memory. "I sort of insisted on it."

Holt got out his makings, sensing that Fool's Eagle had a story that would take time in the telling, sensing as well that this man, despite whatever it was he knew, was not an enemy.

"You heard of the Carlisle Indian Industrial School?"

Holt shook his head no.

"Carlisle, Pennsylvania," Fool's Eagle explained. "Set up by do-gooders to provide a few special redskins with an education beyond what most of us got, which was classes usually taught by some Indian agent's wife who could barely read and cipher herself."

That explained why Fool's Eagle spoke English so well, though Holt was otherwise mystified as to where this was going.

"I was packed off to there about five years back. I did want the learning, but it was a sad and lonely period for me." He shook his head absently at the cigarette Holt offered. "It wasn't too good a time for my wife, either."

Fool's Eagle sighed. "Quint has gussied up the story so it tells more picaresque. He stole my wife about six months before I returned. The Emma Franks woman was not on the scene in those days; she'd never have allowed it."

"She does seem to have some grip over him. Wonder how she manages it."

"Pay attention," Fool's Eagle said, a little sharply. "When my wife's father came after her, Quint shot him in cold blood. He kept my wife locked in a shack hardly bigger than a chicken coop, and brutalized her repeatedly for all that time."

"Sorry," Holt muttered.

"When I returned and learned of this, I waited in ambush outside the shack. He came on the second night. He unlocked the hut and I confronted him. I had a Remington rifle. I meant to give him a chance to draw and then shoot him in the chest, but he charged at me. I was startled and rushed my shot, got him in the jaw instead." He shook his head sardonically. "I'd lost some of my gun skills while I was getting civilized."

Holt lit the cigarette with a branch from the fire.

"My wife was cowering in the shack's corner, and hardly seemed to recognize me. Though it was late, people would have heard the shot. I got her away from there on horseback, riding double behind me. We moved quickly until we were several miles out. It wasn't until then, when we stopped to rest the horse, that I had my first good look at her."

Fool's Eagle's face was stoic, but his eyes were moist. "She was filthy, and gaunt as a skeleton. One of her eyes had been recently blackened, and her front teeth were missing. She shied away from me, and though it was a warm night, she shivered. There was madness in her eyes, but through it she could see how I looked at her."

He gazed at Holt. "I could feel the expression on my face, and I can feel it still, and will always be haunted by it. A few minutes after we reached camp, she got hold of a pistol and used it on herself."

"Jesus," Holt breathed. "And now you and him are trading partners?"

"It suits my purposes," Fool's Eagle said. "When you're a redskin in a white man's world, you learn to be pragmatic."

He paused a moment. "I knew it wasn't over, that I had to remove the threat of revenge from Quint because it would menace all my people. The best way was to give him the opportunity and get it over with.

"After Quint came back with his metal jaw, word went out and arrangements were made. If Quint broke the agreement, he was promised the torching of his town and a full-scale Indian war."

Fool's Eagle pointed across the prairie to the east. "We were there, halfway between Lobo and my people's encampment. A dozen men from town—this was before wolfing—and twice that many Blackfeet braves, but we had fewer guns. Quint and I fought."

Fool's Eagle stared toward where this had happened. "First I was scared and then I was outraged, and I let it possess me and strengthen me. I felt mystically empowered, and I truly believe a spirit possessed me."

He smiled. "Though I could have used a stronger spirit. Like any scared animal, Quint will strike out if his back is forced to the wall. Before it was over, Quint broke my arm and a couple of ribs. And here is an irony: I fractured my hand on his steel plate. Yet when it ended, he lay on his back in the dirt, conscious but too battered to move, and I sat on his chest and held a rock above him in my good hand, and I smashed it down to his face."

Holt stared, enrapt.

"I stopped a fraction of an inch before driving his nose into his brain, and that finished it. My people helped me away and eventually I healed. Quint was not so stupid he didn't realize that something extraordinary had happened, that I'd held him by the heels over a bottomless well in which he could see his own mortality."

Fool's Eagle set another branch on the fire. "It scared him, scared him badly and permanently. When Emma Franks drifted into Lobo, she saw the fear on him like the mark of Cain, and took advantage."

Holt let out his breath. "That's some tale," he said, "and you're some species of Indian."

"Thanks," Fool's Eagle said.

Despite his weariness, Holt felt there was still something to this encounter unresolved in his mind. "You're not here by accident," he guessed.

"I'm here to help. After that you're going to help me."

"Sounds fair," Holt said. "Where do we start?"

"By getting some sleep." Fool's Eagle examined the sky; the moon was up. "I make it about ten o'clock, so we've got plenty of time for shut-eye before we move out."

"To where?"

"Lobo," Fool's Eagle said, "to rescue your woman."

Holt felt as if he'd been kicked in the stomach. So Sam *was* alive, and yet he thought about what Quint had done to Fool's Eagle's wife, this new revelation of the viciousness of which the man was capable . . .

"There's Emma to hold him off," Fool's Eagle said, divining Holt's notions, "and anyway, nothing we can do now."

"Why not?"

"Doesn't fit my plan," Fool's Eagle said.

He wrapped the blanket around him and stretched out on the ground close to the fire. His breathing became regular before a minute had passed.

It took Holt a good deal longer to sleep, and as had been happening lately, he awoke frequently. Each time it was with a jolt, and thoughts of Sam.

Chapter Fourteen

Sam lay on the pallet in the locked cabin, staring into the darkness. The room contained no lamp, nor anything to occupy her if she did have light. She was wide-awake, having dozed on and off again throughout the day and evening, to salubrious effect. Her head and hand both worked again, and she felt vigor, impatience, and more than a little concern.

She got up and went to the tiny window to check her watch in the moon's glow. It was nearly midnight, her thirtieth hour as a prisoner. In that time she'd been given water but nothing to eat, so she was famished, though that was not a major concern. Emma Franks was playing games with her, and damned if Sam understood the rules.

Emma was shrewd enough to know that isolation, hunger, cold, and uncertainty softened up a person—but so did violence or its threat. While Sam had exhibited more than a little courage to Emma, both were aware that anytime Emma wished, she could no doubt compel her to reveal the facts about herself and Holt.

Which led to only one conclusion: Emma already knew.

Another unresolved question came back to her. About midday she'd been awakened from one of her naps by the sound of riders. She could see nothing from the angle of the window, but thought she heard Quint's voice, receding from her. That opened other imponderables, confusing and not comforting.

Sam turned from the window, reexamined the spare furnishing of the room. After a time she went to the table, upended it. It was crudely built, the legs attached only by toed-in nails.

Sam clubbed both hands around one, planted her boot on the upside-down tabletop and began levering the leg loose.

A key scratched at the lock a quarter hour later. Sam snatched up the table leg and sprang to the wall beside the entry, her back flat against it.

The door was kicked open, bounced halfway back. There was no other movement nor sound for a long moment, and then a clunk as something struck the ground. Emma Franks said, "Show yourself."

Sam drew breath, held it, whirled toward the door and swung the makeshift club. Emma darted back, and the tip of the table leg caught the doorjamb. Emma lunged, got both hands around it, jerked it away and flung it outside.

Her eyes burning dully, Emma punched Sam in the jaw.

Sam's knees buckled, but Emma jerked her upright by the shoulders, pushed her backward across the room and threw her on the bed.

"You're not very smart, are you?"

It took time for Sam to refocus her vision, and when she was able, she saw Emma's plain visage, and before it, larger and even more lethal, the muzzle of a revolver.

"For the time being you are worth more to me alive than dead," Emma said. "But not much more."

Emma regarded the three-legged table sourly. "All you are is bait, on the off chance that man of yours does make it out of those mountains. And when he realizes this is the only place you could be, we'll be ready for him."

As if she had lost interest, Emma went out, retrieved the bucket that Sam had heard her drop outside the door. She decanted the water into the pitcher.

"You made up any good tales for me?" Emma said.

"I don't have to." Sam sat up. "I don't know what wrong ideas you've gotten, but—"

"It's true they was only ideas when I decided to let you

go off after Gutt two days ago," Emma interrupted. "Since then they've become facts."

Emma turned to face her. "When you first showed up in these parts, I figured you were a thorn in my side." She grinned. "How was I to know you were actually money in my pocket?"

Sam kept dismay from the steady gaze she returned. "Where did you get that notion?"

Emma continued smiling as she went to the door. "You ponder on that question," she said. "It might help you pass the hours."

"What the hell are we waiting for?" Holt demanded for the third time.

Fool's Eagle pointed across what passed for Lobo's main street. "She's in there."

Holt followed his gaze to the cabin, perhaps thirty feet distant from where he and Fool's Eagle crouched in the shadow of Quint's livery barn. "So let's get her *out* of there," Holt said.

"My wife was pent in that shack," Fool's Eagle said. "What we are going to do is burn it to the ground."

"After we release Sam, I presume," Holt said dryly.

Something moved to Holt's right. He dropped and turned, bringing up the gun already in his hand.

Charity Morgan hunched down beside him. "Here's what you were waiting for." She produced a metal pry bar.

"For God's sake," Holt said with disbelief. "I could have shot off the lock."

"That only happens in dime novels," Fool's Eagle said. "Plus we needed the kerosene."

Holt saw that Charity was also toting a five-gallon jug. "We don't need to burn down the town," Holt said. "You left out a few things, such as that you still got a mad on for Quint."

"Quint isn't here," Fool's Eagle said.

Before Holt could inquire as to where he came by this latest bit of intelligence, Charity said, "The horses, yours

WINTER OF THE WOLF 113

and hers, will be in the barn, so we've got to bust them out."

"Damned straight," Holt said. "I'm not leaving my animals and gear to Quint."

Fool's Eagle's mount, a handsome dappled pinto, was picketed on the range a half mile out, beyond earshot of any random noise—which, Holt decided, would principally come from farting. It was one of the most odoriferously gaseous animals Holt had ever encountered.

"Emma is all we got to worry about, and she's your job," Fool's Eagle said.

The unlikeliness of all of this—Sam within yards of rescue, unanswered questions galore, and his own uncertainty as to just what the hell was going on—was maddening.

"This plan of yours," he said to Fool's Eagle. "Are you about ready to share it with me?"

Holt wedged the pry bar in the space between the shutters of the saloon's front door, then wrapped his bandanna around the whole business. It deadened the noise to a subdued click as he pressed down and the lock plate ripped from the dry planking inside.

"Don't mess up," Charity whispered in his ear. "We need her to entice Quint."

Whatever the hell that meant. Holt paused while she fetched the bar to Fool's Eagle, who applied it to the barn's lock. When Fool's Eagle swung open the double doors, Holt pushed into the barroom.

He stood for a few moments searching for movement and letting his eyes adjust to the darkness. All was still. Holt advanced to the stairs, took them one cautious silent step at a time.

At the top was a short corridor, doors to either side. Holt palmed the knob of the one on the left, turned it. He waited another minute, eased it open.

He faintly made out twin beds, other rough furnishings. He took a step inside. Neither bed was occupied.

A muzzle punched hard into the small of his back. Holt froze, and his own gun was plucked from his hand.

"Dead or alive, is what I heard." Emma Franks's voice was soft in his ear. "Correct me if I'm wrong."

Holt raised his hands. Emma said, "Move off a few steps, then turn around." Holt did as she ordered.

Emma seemed ghostly in the dim light, but the guns in each of her hands were real enough. She waggled them.

"Let's go re-une with that girl of yours," Emma said. "I guess I got me a brace of birds this night."

Sam heard the lock on the cabin door rattle once again. She stood in the middle of the close room, waiting.

More scratching noise preceded the louder sound of metal screws splintering out of wood. The door swung inward to reveal a man—Sam recognized the Indian who'd been with Charity on the prairie, and in fact Charity was there as well, standing behind him. He handed her a crowbar and she disappeared as he entered, carrying a large canister.

"Charity'll have the horses here in a half second. You ready to ride?" He unscrewed the cap on the container, began splashing the liquid inside over the cabin walls. Sam smelled the acrid coal-oil stink.

"My partner—" she said.

"He'll be with us directly. Now move."

Sam exited and he backed out after her, dribbling the last of the kerosene on the doorsill. Sam touched at his shoulder. "Holt—where is he?"

"Look behind you, sweetie," Emma Frank said.

Sam turned carefully. Emma stood halfway between them and the barn, with Holt before her and almost completely concealing her. Holt held his hands up at shoulder level.

"That stink ain't you, is it, Fool's Eagle?" Emma said meanly. "You strike a match, and Mr. Holt here is dead the same moment. The law'll thank me."

Sam took a step toward him, and Holt stiffened as

WINTER OF THE WOLF 115

Emma's gun bore into him. "No one is gonna miss these two, but you at least got a chance, redskin." Emma slung out a hand, and a coil of rope landed between her and Fool's Eagle. "Hog-tie 'em," she ordered.

Fool's Eagle stood his ground.

"It's all over," Emma insisted. "For these two, your pack of savages, and Morgan as well. We win. Only consolation prize for you is your life, you do what I say."

Maybe Sam made some slight movement or expression that gave it away, or maybe Emma was truly prescient. Whatever, Emma whirled suddenly and ducked to one side as Charity came up behind her and swung the crowbar at her.

Emma stepped inside as the blow swept past, bringing the gun up. Holt leaped on her back, grappling for her wrists as Charity half turned with the momentum of her swing. One of Emma's guns went off and dirt puffed at Charity's feet.

Holt rode her down, wrested the weapon away. While he was going for the other, Emma punched him in the face, manic anger powering her strength. Holt scrambled back and Emma jumped to her feet. For a moment she stood there, her arms spread wide, as if welcoming the bullet.

She laughed crazily, turned without a word and stalked away, inviting Holt to back-shoot her.

He could not, of course, and he stumbled off toward Sam. She moved to meet him, came into his arms.

"Later for that," Fool's Eagle snapped. "Get horseback, you two on the bay. Charity, you take the roan."

This was no time for argument. Holt made the saddle, pulled Sam up behind him as Charity mounted up.

Fool's Eagle struck a match and tossed it into the cabin.

The kerosene ignited with an incendiary whoosh, flames exploding from the door as Fool's Eagle jumped back, vaulted onto the roan and grabbed Charity's waist. As the horses danced from the fire, an unholy wail arose.

Emma slammed through the saloon's bat-wing doors, emerged in the space of a heartbeat with a rifle.

Holt drew and shot in her general direction, hollered at Fool's Eagle, "Go!" He fired again, this time aiming inches above her head.

Emma shied to one side. Holt grunted "Hang on" to Sam, took off after Fool's Eagle. A moment before they entered the cover behind the barn, Emma got off a shot, the bullet coming so close that the corner post was splintered, a fleck of it embedding itself in Holt's cheek.

"Too bad," Fool's Eagle said. "I meant to take Emma with us." He shrugged. "But you know what Robert Burns said about the best laid plans of mice and men."

Wondering vaguely what he was on about, Holt swung Sam down, unsheathed his rifle, dismounted and lurched around, scanning their back track. But there was no sign, and really no prudent reason for Emma to give chase, and the half mile of prairie between them and Lobo was empty of movement.

Fool's Eagle unhitched his and Charity's horses from where they were tethered to a clump of scrub brush. Charity took the reins, said, "Otherwise that worked out mostly okay."

Off south, the flames of the burning cabin reached livid fingers toward the sky. "Worked swell," Holt said, "and how about if we skeedaddle."

Sam gave him a loopy, relieved grin that made Holt uncomfortable. She took her horse from Fool's Eagle.

"Now where?" Charity said.

"To San Francisco," Holt snapped. "I hear the opera is in town." He calmed himself. "To the ranch, of course."

Fool's Eagle considered. "Now Quint'll come after you for certain. You might want to camp with my people for a while."

Holt shook his head. "Just as certain, Quint'll take it out on Morgan if I'm not there. We've got to side him, now that we're in this deep."

"I'll ride along." Fool's Eagle glanced at Holt as they

moved out at a fast walking pace. "You remember what I said?"

"You want my help," Holt said. "How so?"

"In due course." He nodded politely at Sam. "The name is Fool's Eagle."

She introduced herself and asked, "Carlisle?"

Fool's Eagle was amused. "You're a good guesser."

"I don't know of any other white man's schools where Indians can learn to talk as you do."

Holt thought that was a brassy comment, but Fool's Eagle merely said, "I'll take that as a compliment."

He rode up ahead to fall in beside Charity, said something to her in a low voice. Charity laughed. Leaving them to whatever was going on, Holt moved up closer to Sam. "Someone has got to be in charge," he said.

"What's that mean?"

"Back up in the mountains. When I said we were riding out . . ."

Sam sat more rigidly in the saddle. "This is the first thing you've got to tell me, now we're together again?"

"It's important."

Sam shook her head firmly. "You've got wrong ideas about how a partnership works—at least this partnership."

Holt marshaled his thoughts. "I'm saying this badly."

"I'll give you a second try."

"What I meant is I was worried about you."

Sam accepted it as an apology. "I'm sorry, too. We were both mule-headed. Let's try to not have it happen again."

"Fine with me."

"What did you do?"

Holt told his tale. By its end, they'd reached the milky river. "I should have left your horse," Sam said.

"No, you did the right thing," Holt contradicted.

Ahead of him Fool's Eagle held up a hand and said, "Quiet."

Holt spun to look behind him, but no one was tagging along. "What is it?"

Fool's Eagle dismounted. "Come on," he said.

Holt handed his reins to Sam and followed Fool's Eagle on foot as he went upstream through the brush lining the river bank. Fool's Eagle moved with effortless silence, but Holt had to concentrate to follow suit.

They'd gone maybe a quarter mile when Fool's Eagle pulled him down into the brush's cover. Five men sat huddled around a fire in a clearing before them though at first Holt could not make out much beyond their shapes. He was wondering how Fool's Eagle had sensed them from such a distance, when one said, "Damned if this isn't cold work."

"Shut up and get some sleep," another said.

Now Holt saw that the men were dressed in buckskins and blankets, much like Fool's Eagle's attire, and had black braided hair. That made them Blackfeet, except for one jarring contradiction.

The two had spoken with the accents of Kentucky, or maybe Texas—in any case, of white men.

Fool's Eagle drew Holt back. "You rejoin the others," Fool's Eagle murmured. "I'll be along directly."

As Holt eased away, he heard a bird call close at hand, incongruous in the wintry surroundings. He held up, watched as Fool's Eagle whistled a second time.

Minutes passed, and then one of the five appeared. He and Fool's Eagle parleyed. Although Holt could not make out the words, he could hear enough to ascertain that neither was speaking English. This Indian, at least, was genuine.

Holt retreated, came eventually to Sam and Charity. Holt shook his head at Sam's inquiring look, and she kept her silence. Fool's Eagle arrived a few minutes later, mounted up and led them downstream.

Holt's curiosity was waxing. "What's this about?"

Instead of answering, Fool's Eagle asked, "When was the last time you had real coffee?"

"Two days back," Holt said.

Fool's Eagle nodded, and Holt looked up to see Morgan's headquarters across the grassland. "We'll have rancher Morgan put on a pot," Fool's Eagle said, "and then we will make medicine."

Chapter Fifteen

Something was clearly on Prospect Morgan's mind as he dished up a breakfast of fried eggs and beefsteaks. It might have been displeasure at Charity's jaunt into town, or the presence of an Indian at the meal, but Holt sensed it was something more. Both the ruddiness that hard drinking brought to Prospect's features and the inchoate scent of apprehension he carried had increased as events moved toward conclusion.

Prospect lingered over the coffeepot when he finished serving, but by now it was too late to much matter to Holt. It appeared there were few left who were not on to his secrets. "You've clammed up," he said to Fool's Eagle.

The Blackfeet savored a piece of beef. "Do you enjoy iroony?"

Holt was trying to remain patient—he did owe Fool's Eagle a lot—but at the moment he wasn't much fetched by his elliptical manner. "To what does that refer?" Holt demanded.

"The man you're seeking, Gutt," Fool's Eagle said. "He came out of the mountains, probably while you were holed up with Geeson. Likely he passed within yards of Geeson's dugout, knowing you were around but not exactly where."

"He does now, assuming you're right." There was a cheering notion, Holt thought. "I want the whole story," Holt demanded, "beginning to end."

Fool's Eagle chewed complacently. "Part is observation, part deduction, and part from what Pretty On Top told me.

WINTER OF THE WOLF

He's the Blackfeet I spoke with this morning, while you watched."

Holt scowled.

Fool's Eagle said, "I expected you'd be there. Never mind; here is how it appears to shape up."

Charity was watching him across the table, as was Stanley Morgan. Holt sensed part of what was about to come was news to the rancher as well.

"You two coming here is what has caused all of this," Fool's Eagle said.

Morgan spoke for the first time. "It would have happened eventually. Better now than later."

"Better for you, maybe," Holt said. "For us, I'm thinking we'd be served by getting the hell out of this territory fast as we can."

As usual, Sam looked to be on the verge of disagreement, and that made Holt feel angry and pressured. She was the one who always pushed for the final resolution of confrontation with Gutt, but it was he who must actually face him.

"I'm not going to bring up old arguments," Sam responded to his gaze, "except to point out that after chasing Gutt across most of the frontier, it'd be a shame to turn tail."

Holt stared at Fool's Eagle. "But it's not just Gutt anymore, is it?"

"He's only one of your many concerns," Fool's Eagle confirmed.

Holt pushed aside his mostly empty plate. "I wonder if I could prevail upon you for more coffee," he said to Prospect. "I reckon I might need it to wash down what I am about to be asked to swallow."

The Blackfeet had always known, Fool's Eagle began, that Quint was behind the rustling and that the phony Indians were wolfers. Fool's Eagle's people had little to do with it.

"What about those two Blackfeet among them this morning?" Holt interrupted.

"I'll get to that," Fool's Eagle said.

At some point between now and the spring, he continued, Quint planned to gather his wolfers into a raiding party and descend on Morgan's headquarters. Prior to the arrival of Holt and Sam, Quint could bide his time and pick his opportunity. Morgan and his brother and niece were outnumbered, and the cows conveniently gathered in the confines of the feed lot, ripe for Quint's picking. On pain of death, the Morgans would be forced to capitulate without a whimper.

While he waited, Quint meant to continue the Indian ruse, and when the final raid came, would likely have witnesses on hand to confirm the "Blackfeet" depredations. This would be sufficient provocation to accomplish Quint's second objective, to drive the natives out along with the Morgans. Quint would not even have to attack the Blackfeet, but only to apply to the Indian Agent, who lived comfortably in Fort Benton and didn't give a fig for his supposed charges. The agency would be compelled by law to relocate the Blackfeet, and Quint would be sole proprietor of all of this country and his town as well.

When Holt and Sam showed up, it skewed Quint's situation and made it significantly more complex. Quint had not achieved his present station as baron of Lobo and king of the wolfers without a good deal of savvy.

"Are we talking of Quint or Emma?" Charity put in at this point.

Fool's Eagle nodded agreement but did not elaborate on her gloss. Still, the issue of the woman's suasion over Quint was one Holt meant to explore further in the near future.

Quint recognized Holt as a man with shootist skills and violent experience. His first guess would naturally be that Morgan had hired himself a gunhand, his first response the effort to beat up Holt badly enough to make him turn tail.

When that did not work, Quint—no doubt under Emma's orders—stepped back to see what he might see. That Holt neither left nor came gunning for him seemed to undermine his original assumption; Holt and Sam could be what they claimed, cowhands employed to bring Morgan's stock in from the range. Their retreat from the rustlers on the last day of the roundup was further confirmation.

Under that reasoning, with the roundup complete Quint expected them to ride out, and he could reimplement his original raiding plan at his leisure. "Maybe you should have left," Fool's Eagle opined. "But too late now."

"We'll see about that," Holt said, rolling cigarettes at the cabin table.

"But next thing that happened, Quint got wind you were looking for Gutt."

"Yeah," Holt said, "thanks to Miss Charity here."

"That's not fair," Charity said with assertiveness. "You've as good as accused me of all sorts of underhanded doings in bandying about your business. I told no one."

"Not even me," Fool's Eagle said.

Prospect frowned at the implicit reference to the Indian's intimacy with his daughter. Holt made a mental note that Prospect held all sorts of grievances, real and imagined and mostly the result of fear and impotence. It was a dangerous combination.

"I found out for you where Gutt's wolfing territory was," Charity continued, "because you wished to know. I also almost got my brains beaten in by Emma Franks while we liberated Sam. I hardly see where that makes me part of some Quint-driven conspiracy."

"She's right, son," Morgan said softly. "It's time for you to sort out your friends from your enemies."

"All right," Holt said sullenly. "So we head for the hills and Gutt, and run into Emma, who seems to be pulling Quint's strings. First off they mean to drive us out, and then—"

"Emma changes her mind," Fool's Eagle finished. "I was watching."

"You get around," Holt said. "Why?"

Fool's Eagle shrugged. "To pass the time."

"Don't fool with me," Holt snapped. "You know what I meant: Why did Emma back Quint off?"

"Two reasons that I can think of," Fool's Eagle said. "First, she didn't have to make any decisions on the spot. She knew where you'd be, at least for the next few days. Second, she can scent profit like a cow can smell water."

It must have struck her first, Fool's Eagle speculated, that if Holt was after Gutt, it was because the big man had a price on his head and Holt was either a lawman, or more probably, a bounty tracker. In that case, she and Quint could let Holt do the hard work and then take Gutt from him for the reward.

But the blizzard changed the calculus of this equation. Not only did it drive Sam into Quint's hands, but it sent Holt to ground long enough for word to reach Gutt.

"Son of a dog," Holt swore. "I was holding out hope that wasn't where this was leading. How'd Gutt find out so quickly?"

"Those mountains seem almost empty of humans," Fool's Eagle said, "but there are wolfers everywhere. They can be as stealthy as the animals they seek to eradicate, but they know each other's whereabouts. It is like a telegraph with many branches, each man passing word to two others, until the whole front knows Quint's orders or any other fact of interest. All Gutt needed to learn was that a man and woman were after him, and it wouldn't take him three guesses to figure out who."

Holt's gaze narrowed. "Rein up. I thought I heard you say you didn't know my business?"

"It's not that hard to figure out the rough outline." Fool's Eagle returned Holt's look unflinchingly. "I'd judge that you and your partner are guilty of no crime, which means, if you want Gutt, that he is. My next guess is that you are neither some undercover spy for the law nor a mercenary manhunter. That would have to mean that Gutt has wronged you personally."

"You're a good guesser," Sam said.

Fool's Eagle's explication put Holt in a funk. He forced

himself to pay attention as the Blackfeet picked up its thread.

Like all Indians, Fool's Eagle said wryly, he could melt into nature. He'd seen Sam arrive in Lobo, and noted her failure to emerge from the town. Early the next morning, Gutt rode out of the Rock Creek drainage and made for Lobo, and that night Holt emerged, though he was not the last. That morning while they were liberating Sam, a band of at least a half-dozen wolfers rode toward town.

Holt interrupted with another question. "I was called differently at birth," Fool's Eagle replied. "Part of why I took my present name is my good eyesight. I spotted the wolfers as we rode out."

"Vision of an eagle," Holt said. "How did 'Fool's' get to be part of your moniker?"

"I wonder," Fool's Eagle said blandly. "Maybe because now and then I trust a white man?" he suggested.

Gutt was no stranger to the Blackfeet, Fool's Eagle continued. In his hatred of Indians, Quint considered them superstitious heathens who would cow at the sight of a white man like Gutt. But Fool's Eagle headman, Pete Matt, had gone through enough horrors at white hands—from "civilizing" and a renaming by Jesuit missionaries, to random violence from settlers, to several forced relocations "for the good of his people"—that in his elder years he'd developed a resigned courage.

Not long before Holt and Sam rode to these parts, Gutt delivered an ultimatum from Quint. The Blackfeet could rattle hocks on out of Quint's domain, or they could join him to drive out Morgan, in exchange for which Quint would leave them to their devices.

Pete Matt recognized the second choice as a lie, but a few of the younger and more hotheaded Indians urged siding with Quint. Pete Matt would have no truck with this, and ordered Gutt away. He went, but Pretty On Top and the other Indian that Holt and Fool's Eagle had seen camped with the wolfer rustlers on the milky river left camp with him.

That afternoon, a good six hours before Holt encountered Fool's Eagle for the first time, Gutt and Quint left as well—from Lobo, riding south.

"To where?" Holt asked.

"Fort Benton, I'd say."

Sam got it before Holt. "To send a telegram."

"Yes."

Sam gazed at Holt. "I suppose we can guess to whom he is wiring."

"Clennon Pert," Holt said miserably.

Morgan offered a quizzical look. "The U.S. Federal Marshal sworn to bring us to justice," Holt explained.

"Why would Gutt give you to Quint when you are worth money to anyone who apprehends you?" Morgan asked.

"Gutt can't risk trying to collect," Holt said. "He knows that in Utah we had the chance to talk with Pert before we managed to duck him."

In response to Fool's Eagle's look, Holt said, "Long story. Suffice to say that what you've already figured out is on the mark. I went to prison for a crime Gutt committed, and Sam here is wanted for busting me out. We're worth eight thousand dollars all told."

"We told Pert the true story," Sam picked up, "and I think he believed us enough that if we died in Gutt's vicinity, Pert would look on him with suspicion. That gives us our one edge on the big man: Gutt can't afford to be tied too closely to us."

Holt slurped down the last of his coffee. "On the other hand, Gutt would love to see us put away, whether he gets any of the reward or not. Us arrested solves all his problems."

"You could tell what you know," Charity said.

Morgan shook his head. "Holt is already convicted for the crime, and Miss Lowell is in way over her head. Gutt is safe from their testimony."

Sam's eyes were soft with thought. "Gutt has told Quint and Emma Franks all about us. Quint plans to collect the reward the easy way, by giving us to Pert." She looked up.

"Why did Quint need Gutt with him on the trip to wire Pert?"

"To keep Gutt from changing his mind and killing you himself," Fool's Eagle said.

"Or more likely," Charity put in, "because Quint is afraid to be abroad without protection. Why do you think he's holed up in his town all the time?"

"I don't know," Holt said, "and he wasn't so cowardly when he was whaling the tar out of me."

Sam seemed inordinately interested in this debate, but Holt was more taken with current contingencies. "In case I do decide to saddle up about three seconds from now, tell me what I'm going to miss," he said.

"Could be Quint's stationed some of his boys around to make sure you don't," Fool's Eagle said.

"Could be I'll take my chances," Holt said darkly.

"What's the rest of Quint's plan?" Sam put in.

"Pert gets you, with the help of deputized wolfers, if necessary," Fool's Eagle said. "Soon as he hauls you off, Quint follows through and drives out Mr. Morgan, and after that the Blackfeet."

Holt sighed. "Here is the part where you are going to tell me how I can help you," he surmised.

"And help yourself in the process," Fool's Eagle confirmed.

Holt ground out his cigarette, stared at Sam. "I'm not going to provoke another scene like the one that got us separated in the mountains. But I am going to argue for retreat in favor of a better battlefield."

Sam smiled grimly and said without edge, "Won't happen."

Holt worked on an answer. None came. In frustration he slammed his palm down on the table.

Holt looked around. Everyone sat still, awaiting his tirade, Sam's response.

"I'll tell it for you," Holt said to Sam. "We're staying because it's our best chance to get Gutt, though I don't suppose you have any swell ideas about eluding Clennon Pert in the process."

Sam nodded.

"Then you are going to say," Holt went on, "that Mr. Morgan here has been decent to us even knowing who we are, and we owe him, even if he does have a boozy brother and his addled niece on his hands."

Charity rolled her eyes. "This what you always do?" she demanded. "Lash out when you're cornered? Well, maybe it will come in handy."

Holt ignored her. "Next," he told Sam, "you're going to try to appeal to my better nature, say that if we don't help, Quint wins. With Pert taking us out of the picture, Gutt remains free, while Morgan and the Indians are driven out or slaughtered."

Holt shut up abruptly. Everyone was looking at him or Sam, and it struck him that this must sound not unlike a lovers' spat. "Does that about cover it?" he concluded lamely.

"Pretty much."

"Then I suppose it's time for one of my famous plans," Holt said.

"I'd say so," Sam said.

Chapter Sixteen

"How you holding up?" Fool's Eagle asked.

"Well, let's see," Holt said. "Since this adventure began, I got my nose broke by Quint, I spent enough time chasing cows that my butt wouldn't mind if it never touched another saddle, and before that phase was over, I came near to freezing off my toes. Speaking of toes, the swelling is down after my little fifteen-mile hike."

Holt unlatched the gate to one of Morgan's stock pens. "That's not counting the almosts—almost broke my ankle, almost perished in the blizzard, almost got beat up a second time by a wolfer my partner decided to plug in the thigh, almost got shot by Emma Franks." Holt swung the gate past Fool's Eagle. "Did I leave anything out?"

"Almost about to risk your life helping me and Morgan," Fool's Eagle said.

"Right," Holt said. "Thanks for reminding me."

"You'll come out okay," Fool's Eagle said. "I sense you have luck."

Holt looked at him. "Just what I need at the moment—mystic Indian nonsense."

Fool's Eagle smiled pleasantly, and truth to tell, Holt liked him—and more important, trusted him—quite a bit. The Blackfeet had been through some tough times of his own. Holt entered the pen and moved among the fat cows, uncoiling the rope he carried. "How many does etiquette require?"

Morgan had nearly popped his cork at breakfast when Holt requested he give up cows for a gift to the Blackfeet.

Prospect was, perplexingly, even more wroth. "They steal your stock, and you're gonna reward them?" "That's settled," Charity replied hotly. But Prospect stubbornly refused to accept that the rustling was Quint's doing. Holt wondered why he was defending the man.

When Morgan balked, Holt laid down the law: If he was committing himself to this business, Morgan would do it his way. Morgan finally agreed to four head.

"Two are enough, but fat and meaty," Fool's Eagle told Holt in the barnyard. "It will mollify Morgan, and lessen his dismay at our little surprise."

Holt looked at him sharply. "What surprise might that be?"

"I'll fill you in by and by."

Holt saw to his chore; the smell of the cows was unsettling his breakfast. He pushed the rump of one out of the way to get to the head of a beefy beast that was burrowing gluttonously into a pile of hay. Holt got his arm under the animal's neck and yanked it upright. It shook free and Holt stumbled a step backward, planting his boot firmly in the center of a pile of fresh droppings.

That provoked laughter. Holt spun angrily, but it was Sam, who had appeared at the gate beside Fool's Eagle. Holt worked the rope's noose out, looped it over the cow's head, and took out his irritation dragging the cow from the corral.

He took another rope from the fence post, thrust it at Sam and said, "Your turn."

She accepted it as a challenge and plunged into the shifting mass of beeves, making her way to a likely candidate. Over her shoulder she said, "This one okay?"

The animal shoved her in the back with its snout, and Sam fell to her hands and knees in the snow and ordure.

"Why not?" Holt said dryly. "Now you owe it one."

They set out from the ranch at mid-morning, with the weather continuing to demonstrate headstrong changes. If not for the cold, which had moderated to not many degrees below freezing, the sky would have belonged more to summer than winter. The clouds were black with potential storm, yet large openings among them were pure blue, so that patches of sunlight darted about the prairie like ephemeral gremlins. One moment they were bathed in a sunbeam, so bright off the snow that Holt had to squint against its glare; another moment they rode into near-twilight shadow, as if passing through a curtain separating a chandeliered chamber from a dim hallway.

At a rise that would put the ranch headquarters out of sight to their backs, Holt turned in the saddle. He expected to see Charity, and indeed she stood before the outermost pen, watching them.

"You and her," Sam said.

"What?" Holt sounded defensive. "I haven't given the slightest encouragement to any overtures."

Fool's Eagle laughed. "You can turn a phrase now and then," he said. "Miss Lowell was talking to me."

"Call me Sam."

Fool's Eagle turned comically sober, raised a hand with palm toward her and intoned solemnly, "How, Sam." He bowed in the saddle. "That is the way we redskins say 'howdy,' at least in the dime novels."

Sam smiled back. "You're telling me to mind my own business," she said. "Okey-doke."

Back at Morgan's, Charity had appeared at about the point where they got the two cows tethered to Holt's and Fool's Eagle's saddle horns and were preparing to head out. "Can I come?" she asked Fool's Eagle.

"Not a good idea. You know how my father feels, and if you confirm what he suspects, he's liable to stake you out, smear you with honey, and let the bears have you."

"There's no bears until spring," Charity said.

"He'll wait," Fool's Eagle said.

Her expression indicated she knew he was fooling with her, but also that the teasing was metaphor for some true aspect of the situation. Anyway it was enough to make her drop her petition to accompany them.

On the prairie Holt said, "Is she and you why Prospect wants to believe the Blackfeet are the thieves?"

"I think there's more to it than that." He hesitated. "I didn't want to burden you, but Prospect has been seen in Quint's company. Even Charity doesn't know."

"Just what we need," Holt muttered.

They reached the bottom of the hillock, where another of the sunlit patches surrounded them. Instantly the air felt twenty degrees warmer, enough that Holt was almost uncomfortable in his thick coat. He considered removing it, but before he could complete the thought they were in chilly shadow again. Wind came up, and the dark clouds sailed more quickly across the sea of blue on which they appeared to float.

"She is willful and so am I," Fool's Eagle said after a while. "We became close."

Despite previous evidence of the relationship, Holt started. "You mean you and her . . . ?"

Fool's Eagle looked at him. "Our proctors at Carlisle were fond of raising theories regarding miscegenation. You wouldn't subscribe to them, would you?"

Holt was confused. "What are we talking about?"

"Intermingling of the races," Sam explained.

Holt got it. "I'm broad-minded," he declared.

"Wish I could say the same for the chief." Fool's Eagle scanned the horizon. "Shouldn't be more than a few hours before we reach camp." He shook his head, as if the prospect of arrival had its negative side. "First thing I'm likely going to hear from him is about Charity."

"This Pete Matt is your father?"

Fool's Eagle nodded.

"So that makes you sort of a prince," Holt said.

Sam snorted derisively. "For goodness' sake, Holt. You spend all your life on the frontier, and you still take your notions of Indian society from storybooks."

"I haven't had so much truck with natives," Holt muttered.

"You are about to get your first lesson," Fool's Eagle

WINTER OF THE WOLF 133

said. But he didn't seem too put out at Holt's naive misstep, and looked to be about to add some comment.

As he opened his mouth, the serenity of the day exploded.

A rifle went off and a slug whined past. Fool's Eagle drew his handgun and fired two quick shots ahead and off to the left.

Holt caught a glimpse of metal reflecting in one of the pockets of sunlight, well out of pistol range. He launched himself from the saddle and caught Sam around the middle, throwing himself and her from horseback to land hard in the snow.

The rifle fired and the pinto whinnied in instant agony. It tried to rear, and Fool's Eagle let loose of it, hit the ground just ahead of where Holt and Sam were entangled. The pinto gasped and collapsed, its bulk missing them by inches. As it rolled, they had to scuttle back to avoid its flailing hooves.

In the few seconds it took for the horse to run out of strength and lie gasping and twitching, Fool's Eagle was on the move. The bay and roan milled half panicked nearby, unable to bolt because of the drag of the cows tethered to their saddle horns.

Holt pulled Sam to the pinto for cover against this sudden ambush. A bullet hole dimpled the horse's gut, and blood flecked the spittle it ejected with each laboring breath. For a moment that was the only sound, and then Fool's Eagle said, "I am in no mood to be pinned down by some peckerwood."

As he rose, Fool's Eagle pulled his knife with his left hand, the pistol still in his right. He vaulted onto Sam's roan, slashed the rope to free it from the cow's burden, and when the knife was resheathed, drew Sam's Winchester and tossed it down to her.

Almost presciently, Fool's Eagle danced the roan sideways as another rifle shot whistled through the space he had occupied a moment earlier. He lay low on the roan's mane and charged in the direction of their attacker.

"Shoot the pinto in the temple," Holt ordered Sam, "then stay put and cover us." By then he was following Fool's Eagle's example. He made it to the bay, kept it between him and the threat while he cut the tether, got aboard, and raced after Fool's Eagle.

Behind him he heard the shot that put the pinto out of its agony. Fool's Eagle fired three more times. He wasn't likely to hit anything, but the intimidation of the fusillade, and perhaps the surprise of his reckless head-on assault, gave pause to the rifleman.

Staying low, Holt worked his own long gun from its scabbard. As it came free, Fool's Eagle fired once more. Holt swore and reined to a skithering stop, the bay almost losing its footing on the snow-slicked grass.

The ambusher sprang to his feet, levered his rifle and raised it to his shoulder. Fool's Eagle was nearly upon him, a looming target to the man. Holt was still a hundred yards distant.

Holt sighted, fired, and missed, but by a narrow enough margin to get the man's attention.

Fool's Eagle reached him, and like a bulldogger in a roping contest, dove from his horse to throw his full weight atop him. The man tried to crab away. Fool's Eagle flipped him on his back with no more effort than it might take to turn a baby for changing, then pinned the man's arms with his knees.

As Holt caught up, the man tried to spit, but no longer had the breath. Saliva dribbled down his jaw.

Fool's Eagle punched him in the face, bloodying his nose. He shoved the muzzle of his handgun up under the soft flesh beneath the man's chin.

"You're empty," the man sneered.

This struck Holt as a particularly moronic bit of bluster, given the man's present circumstances.

Fool's Eagle feigned dismay. The man grinned stupidly.

Fool's Eagle slammed the gun's barrel against the side of his head. The man went limp, slumped on the ground leadenly.

Fool's Eagle made an elaborate show of unlatching the cylinder of his revolver, dumping the six empty shell cases into his palm. "I believe you are right," he said to the inert form beneath him, "you horse-killing son of a bitch."

Their attacker remained unconscious while Holt finished trussing his wrists and ankles with the remnants of the rope he'd removed from the saddle horn. He rose to holler out to Sam that everything was taken care of, but when he looked back, the prairie was empty save for the fallen pinto.

"Here she comes," Fool's Eagle said.

From the opposite direction, Sam was riding toward them on what Holt took to be the attacker's horse. If he was becoming accustomed to her ignoring his orders, he was still less than resigned, and to Fool's Eagle he said with irritation, "Didn't they teach you to count at that Carlisle school?"

"I knew I'd fired six times," Fool's Eagle said, "but I also knew you'd watch over me. Your luck rubs off." The man stirred and opened his eyes. "Anyway," Fool's Eagle said to him, "I've reloaded now." He trained his gun on the man.

The man blinked, came fully around, and grinned. "You figure a redskin can kill a white man and walk away?" he blustered.

Here is an hombre who was last in line when common sense was doled out, Holt thought with disgust. The man went on grinning when Holt advanced on him with his own gun drawn. "I'm not a redskin," Holt said.

"I know who you are," the man sneered.

Holt put a bullet into the snow a few inches from his ear. The man screamed. "Time to get down to business," Holt snapped. He hoped that the shot's concussion hadn't burst the man's eardrum; he needed him able to hear. "What's your name?" he tried.

The man's smart-mouthed sap was beginning to drain. "Doake," he said. "Name is Doake."

There was no need to follow up with inquiry as to this Doake's profession; if the clothing had not given it away, the stench would have. Doake wore what Holt had come to think of as the wolfers' uniform: buffalo robe over greasy denim britches and broken-down boots; a full beard, and long scraggly hair so dirty it might not have made soap's acquaintance since the war.

"And who am I?" Holt said.

Doake gazed at him for a time before shrugging elaborately. Holt crouched and tapped him on the side of the head with the gun. "Jeez, but you are a slow learner," Holt said. He peered down at the man. "Where have I seen you?"

The seriousness of Doake's situation was at last beginning to sink in. "In Yuma."

"What were you in for?"

Doake managed to sit up. "General brutality."

Maybe the man truly was dim, Holt thought. "Tell me what I wish to know."

"Couple of months back, before I come up here for the wolfing season," Doake said, "I saw the poster on you, so's I knew you'd busted out. Then you walk into Quint's saloon, t'other week before the snows came."

"Then why'd you save your move until now?"

Doake tried to find a position that would accommodate his bonds more comfortably. "You wouldn't by any chance consider untying me?"

"Correct," Holt answered. "Answer the question."

"Eight thousand is a lot of money," Doake said, "but I had premonitions." He moved his arms best as he could. "Guess they come true."

Fool's Eagle turned and stalked to where Doake sat. "Maybe you are a coward. Takes a coward to shoot from ambuscade, kill a man's horse."

"Maybe you're right," Doake said. "But I overcome it when I got the word and come into town and Quint is gone. There's talk that indicates at least some are figuring out who you are. This notion developed that I could beat the rest to you." Doake grimaced ruefully. "I reckon greed clouded my judgment."

Holt rose to his feet and paced, then turned back. "What the hell do we do with him?"

"Gimme my horse and I'll ride out of these parts," Doake suggested. "You'll never see me again."

"You don't have a horse," Fool's Eagle snapped.

It wasn't much of a trade for the pinto. The wolfer's animal was rib-skinny and spotted with mange; figure on one such as Doake to have little regard to his transport.

"I've got no qualms about killing him," Fool's Eagle went on, "but I expect you'll take exception. How about if we leave him as he is?"

"Good as killing him," Sam said. "Cut him loose. It'll take him the rest of the day to make Lobo, and whatever harm he can do us is already done."

"Isn't that swell," Holt muttered. "How fine the fates have been treating us."

In disgust he crouched again, slit Doake's bonds with little care, and took grim and childish satisfaction when his knife nicked the wolfer's palm. "Shouldn't have done that," Doake said darkly, as if he had the upper hand once more.

Holt kicked him in the butt as he stood. "Get the hell away from me." He went to his horse, was about to put his foot in the stirrup when he caught movement from the corner of his eye.

Holt spun, his hand slapping for his gun butt. Doake was bent to his boot, and from it emerged a wickedly curved wolfing knife.

Holt caught sight of something else, Fool's Eagle off to one side, watching this scene unfold but making no motion to take a hand.

Doake drew back his arm, holding the knife by the blade, his eyes beady and drilling into his target, Holt's chest.

Holt pulled his gun free, dropped away and to one side.

Sam shot Doake in the stomach. The wolfer stared wide-eyed, stumbled but did not fall. His arm came down and the knife flew at Holt, who twisted and ducked as the knife missed, so he was oriented toward Sam as she put another bullet into Doake's torso.

In the time before any of them moved, the wind came up, moving close to the ground and dusting snow over Doake's inert form. Holt looked up, saw that the patches of sunlight had been blotted out by uniform cover, dark and promising another storm. He felt angry, embarrassed, and worst of all, unsure, and the odd look Fool's Eagle was favoring him with did not help. Sam came up beside him, her face reflecting genuine concern—which nettled him all the more.

Holt gestured at Doake, bleeding into the snow. "That solves one problem," he said, "though it doesn't much address the big picture."

Sam touched at his arm tentatively, as if she almost feared he might turn on her. "Come on," she said gently. "We've got business to see to."

The snowfall when it began was fitful, but now it came in gusts, flakes stinging Holt's face. It fueled anger mixed with guilt. Everywhere he and Sam went, people seemed to get killed. Deserved or not, it was the sort of dire event that weighted a man's conscience.

Beside him as they rode on, Sam said, "It's okay."

Holt turned on her. "What's okay?"

"That you hesitated. It doesn't mean you're scared."

One of the two beeves they were now trailing without benefit of rope veered left. Fool's Eagle rode after it, a convenient excuse to put himself discreetly out of earshot.

"I'm messing this up," Sam said. "I'm trying to tell you that if you saw taking life like taking one more drink, I'd not abide it. I did what I had to, but I was reluctant, too. It's all that separates them from us."

Holt thought he understood what she was trying to get across, but for the life of him could not dig up a coherent response. Instead he rode ahead to Fool's Eagle, mainly to change the subject so he could rid his mind of it. But what came out when he reached the Blackfeet was, "I got shot in the back in the war. I guess I ended up gun-shy."

Fool's Eagle gave him a thoughtful look. "Not that you haven't fired on a man when you had to."

"This another Indian mind-reading trick?"

"I'm a good judge of an hombre," Fool's Eagle said. "You'll come through when necessary."

Fool's Eagle had anyway read him right. He had killed once since Sam had gotten him out of Yuma, a man named Cavan in the high country of Utah. Snow had covered the ground that time as well, and Holt lay in it with a bullet hole in his flank and afraid of dying, afraid enough to put three quick shots into Cavan's middle. No one ever really won a gunfight, and that incident was a good example. As if he'd hardly been a part of it, Holt saw the scene in his mind's eye from a detached point of view, he and Cavan sprawled and punctured, their blood bubbling into the snow's deathly embrace. . . .

"Damn it," Holt said aloud.

Fool's Eagle looked at him.

"Never mind," Holt said. "How about if we get back to that surprise you mentioned."

"Probably a good idea," Fool's Eagle said judiciously. "I don't want you looking awkward in front of my father."

Pete Matt skinned back the lips of one of the cows and examined its teeth like a dentist checking for decay. He walked around the animal, running his hands over its ribs and flanks, pinching at the flesh to gauge its meatiness. He muttered to no one in particular.

"He says Stanley Morgan is a skilled beef grower," Fool's Eagle translated.

"It's supposed to be a gift," Holt said. "He's acting more like he's considering a purchase."

Pete Matt glanced at Holt before returning his critical eye to the cow. He nodded his approval at last, drew a knife, and without further ceremony cut a deep, long gash across the animal's throat.

Blood spurted three feet into the air, though not a fleck hit the chief. The cow went down as if it were sledgehammered, did not move a muscle. Women came forward and went to work as if they knew what they were about. One slit the belly and began to dry out the guts, another tended to skinning, while a third yanked out the tongue like it was a length of yard goods and lopped it off.

Pete Matt spoke again. "You are invited to the feast," Fool's Eagle said.

"I was already getting used to the idea we'd be spending the night," Holt said glumly. Again Pete Matt gave him a look.

"Be polite," Sam said in a low voice.

Although Holt remembered her earlier admonition when he'd applied his European preconceptions to Fool's Eagle's station as the chief's son, he couldn't help but observe the similarity of the layout of the Blackfeet camp to any other village. The tent from which Pete Matt had emerged on their arrival was larger than the others, the town hall. It fronted on the open area where the cow was being butchered, a sort of public square around which the other tents were arranged in radiating circles. The livery was a long rope strung between two cottonwoods to which a couple dozen horses were tethered, downwind from the residential area. There was even a mercantile of sorts, or at least a storehouse, an open-flapped tent within which Holt spotted baskets of root vegetables and dinner-plate-sized slabs of dried meat.

The woman in charge of eviscerating the cow dug her arm into its belly and came out with a brown quivering slab. She presented it to Pete Matt, who held it in both palms and raised it to the sky, murmuring some incantation.

"He saying grace?" Holt asked, a bit sarcastic.

Pete Matt wiped the blood from his knife on the snow, cut three good-sized slices from the organ. The woman took the remainder back, and Pete Matt advanced on them, where they sat on a blanket before his tent. The chief nodded his head, thrust one of the slices at Holt.

"As a matter of fact, he was," Fool's Eagle said. "It's an appetizer."

Holt accepted the slimy morsel gingerly. Pete Matt gave the other slices to Sam and his son. "Liver helps keep your blood strong," Fool's Eagle said.

"My blood is strong enough already."

Pete Matt surprised Holt: he smiled. Holt glanced at Sam, who also seemed amused.

She bit off some liver and chewed vigorously, went on smiling. There was nothing for it but to eat, and Holt did. It was warm and a little too close to being alive for Holt's druthers, but tasted rich and not unpalatable.

Pete Matt crossed his legs and lowered himself to another blanket that faced them. After that he sat motionless, gazing steadily at Holt with hardly a blink. Sam finished her liver and said to Pete Matt, "That was good. Thank you."

"Make a gesture, like rubbing your tummy or something, so he knows what you're saying," Holt suggested.

"Shut up and eat your liver," Sam said.

Holt did as he was told. Nothing was going to happen until Pete Matt decided the moment was right. At least the main meal was in the works; over in the center of the common area, the women were building a fire, as the cow-butchering got down to the finer work of spitting chunks of beef for roasting.

The camp was a couple of miles beyond any of the range Holt and Sam had covered while gathering Morgan's cows, and a good dozen north of the rancher's headquarters. By the time they'd arrived a half hour previous, it was late afternoon. From a distance as they rode in, Holt thought he saw sign of a goodly fire.

The cloud turned out to be steam. This place, which Fool's Eagle explained served as a semipermanent winter settlement, was at the foot of a smaller subrange of the Rockies, well-timbered with ponderosa and lodgepole pine. A steep creek, another tributary of the milky river, cascaded over boulders through a rock-walled canyon that ended at the camp's upstream boundary, where a hot springs produced what Holt had taken as smoke.

It was a well-chosen situation, Holt had to acknowledge, with water, plenty of driftwood to feed the fire that several of the women were now working to build, and the shelter of the mountains against more extreme weather, yet exposed to plenty of whatever sunlight might emerge. Pete Matt's people looked to Holt's eye to be healthy and well-provisioned; Holt reckoned there were about fifty residents. The women wore long buckskin gowns that draped over high boots of tanned leather, and woven shawls that, like the blankets on which they sat, Holt figured to be trade goods. Most of the men were dressed much like Fool's Eagle, and his father, the chief, was adorned with a necklace made of a leather thong on which sapphires were strung.

Pete Matt went on staring while Holt ate the last of his liver. The chief's appearance, like his son's, gave little hint to his age. He'd have to be at least fifty, Holt reasoned, but his face was smooth-skinned and ungrizzled, and his long hair, hanging in two greased braids over his shoulders, was dark with no hint of gray.

His eyes were equally dark, and Holt had the uncomfortable feeling they were boring into him as the minutes passed. Holt recalled a story Sam told him one time on the trail, about a man's eyes being the pathway to the soul.

Holt licked his fingers. Pete Matt spoke suddenly, a string of sentences in his language. Holt glanced at Fool's Eagle.

"He says you have a good appetite," Fool's Eagle interpreted. "He guesses you have appetite for your woman as well."

Holt felt instantly embarrassed and turned to Sam. She was smiling beatifically at Pete Matt.

"He is pretty sure you are a good man," Fool's Eagle went on, "if something of a queer duck."

"I'm a queer duck!" Holt echoed. "Who is it that decided the best way to spend this evening is sitting on blankets having a stare-down contest?"

Sam elbowed him in the ribs, sharply enough to hurt. Holt said, "Hey!" which got him a second shot in the gut. In exasperation, Holt drew his pouch, gestured elaborately with it at Pete Matt and said, "I have tobacco."

Pete Matt put on an expression of delight that was almost comical. "Well, there's one thing we have in common," Holt said sourly. "We both like our smokes."

As he rolled tobacco within paper, Holt saw Sam and Fool's Eagle exchange a cryptic glance. "What are you two on about?" Holt demanded as he licked the cigarette closed.

He got no answer, though their demeanors suggested they were enjoying a joke to which he was not privy. Hell with it, Holt decided. He held the cigarette in front of his lips, mimed exaggerated inhaling, and offered it to Pete Matt.

The chief took it, examined it with as much thoughtfulness as he had the cow before slaughter, finally placed it between his lips.

"Thank you," Pete Matt said. "Do you have a match?"

Pete Matt had lapsed into another of the long motionless silences he'd evinced since demonstrating, several hours earlier, that he spoke English as well as Holt. That was fine; Holt was belly-full of beefsteak and tubers, and willing to pretend that all was right with his world, at least until morning reawakened him to reality.

Holt sat slumped on a rock submerged below steaming water, near the bank of the creek where it flowed out of the canyon. Here winter was banished; despite that November was well on its course, indeed that snow continued to fall, the canyon side above him was slick rock glazed with spring-green lichen.

The steamingly hot water depended from a fissure in the granite at a rate of no more than a vigorous trickle, but the Blackfeet had built a sort of reservoir from river boulders to form a bathing spot. A couple of yards before Holt, icy, chill water cascaded past; here in this retreat, the hot seep made a pool hot enough to make him wince when he lowered himself into it a few minutes earlier.

Now he reclined up to his neck, a cigarette dangling from his lips and his hat brim pulled low. Pete Matt sat in his passivity to one side, Fool's Eagle to his other. The steam of the hot spring smelled slightly sulfurous, but the overall effect was soporific and infinitely relaxing.

"If I fall asleep," Holt said drowsily, "someone jerk my head above water."

"I will."

Holt tried to leap to his feet, slipped on the pool's bottom instead, heard the hiss as his smoke was dowsed. He came up sputtering, his Stetson floating like a kid's boat next to his shoulder.

A steep switchback path led down to the pool, and Sam stood at its top. Holt got his feet under him, was about to flee toward who knew where, and then remembered that, like Pete Matt and Fool's Eagle, he was bathing stark naked. He hunched back into the water and said, "Go away."

Sam bowed her head at Pete Matt. He studied her, then made a welcoming gesture.

Sam came down the trail to the edge of the pool. Though the night remained mostly clouded, as luck would have it, the moon peered through a breach in the cover. It was illumination enough for Holt to see her start to work loose the buttons of her shirt.

Holt looked away, only to observe that Pete Matt was complacently enjoying whatever was going on behind his back. Water splashed, and Sam settled in close by. Holt could not help himself; he looked. She was stripped down to her chemise, which clung wetly and alluringly to her figure.

"You are an idiot," she said pleasantly.

"Several times over," Holt managed. "You are talking about what exactly?"

"You don't pay attention. Fool's Eagle mentioned that Chief Matt was educated by Jesuits. You didn't figure that speaking English was part of the indoctrination?"

This issue was on the back burner of Holt's concerns. He risked another glance, in time to see her pull the wet undergarment off over her head.

"Earlier today," Fool's Eagle said broadly, "you mentioned something about being gun-shy."

Holt made himself small under the water and worked to let its influence calm him. "That's enough japery at my expense," he said, carefully keeping his gaze on Fool's Eagle.

From the corner of his eye he noted that Pete Matt continued to regard Sam with frank approval. Holt took another peek. Sam was up to her chin in the water, and with the steam and darkness, there wasn't much to see—though Holt's imagination was working a mile a minute.

Fool's Eagle cleared his throat. "You should know something of Blackfeet history. It is not entirely pretty."

Holt told his imagination to go away and made himself pay attention.

"Prior to the coming of Europeans, and for some years after, we were a war-making tribe. For example, down south of here, on the edge of the town of Missoula, there is a canyon called the Hellgate. It got its name because there the Blackfeet used to ambush and rob Salish, Nez Perce, Coeur d'Alenes."

"You held up other tribes?" Sam asked. "Why?"

Fool's Eagle shrugged. "That was the way it always had been. When white men began to occupy our lands, we fought them as well, though not for long. This was about the time I was born, so I'm talking from lore not experience."

"Something I've been wondering about." Sam's voice drifted lazily on the billows of mist. "Most all of the Indians in this country are on reservations. How did you avoid that?"

"The credit goes to my father, Fool's Eagle's grandfather and the chief before me," Pete Matt answered.

"There's a common conception that western Indians were taken by surprise when Europeans began settling beyond the Mississippi," Fool's Eagle said. "That's nonsense. My ancestors knew as early as the 1600s that the East had been settled. Word traveled from tribe to tribe, and while there might have been some distortions, the gist of what was occurring—our continent being occupied by colonialists—was common knowledge."

"As was the fact that no tribe had prevailed against them," Pete Matt said. "Although we did resist with arms now and again, my father quickly saw that our fate would be the same as every other people's. He determined to make the best of the inevitable."

"Other tribes were taken in by the blandishments of the government," Fool's Eagle said, "including some bands of Blackfeet. My grandfather signed treaties as well, and we gave up many of our traditional lands, such as the area near Missoula. But in trade-off he proposed to move up here, where at the time Europeans weren't much interested in the land, and in no treaty did he accept a reservation."

"Eventually, I suppose, we must," Pete Matt said. "I was hoping it would not happen while I was chief." He sighed. "Times change faster than you expect."

That certainly applied to his own life lately, Holt thought. "But you still figure you can slow it down," he said.

Pete Matt remained silent for a spell. "Like my father before me, I believe in destiny," he said finally.

"You mean you are ready to petition for a reservation while there is still land available?" Sam asked.

"I was speaking of you," Pete Matt said, "you and your man. That which perhaps must happen can nevertheless be put off for a while. The destiny of this season is that you are sent to help."

"I believe in God," Holt said, "but I don't think I'm His instrument."

Pete Matt nodded slowly. "I've given a lot of thought to our situation. You've come to understand part of it, Fool's Eagle tells me."

"And we're sympathetic," Sam said, "but—"

Pete Matt raised a hand, ghostly white in the hot spring's clouds. "Stanley Morgan and my people have gotten along

WINTER OF THE WOLF

over the years, and can so continue. We've also remained largely unmolested by Quint. But now, for whatever reason—long-term resentment over what my son did to him, the urging of the Franks woman, pure greed—he means to drive out Stanley Morgan and us in the bargain."

"Maybe we can stop him, maybe not," Fool's Eagle said. "That depends largely on you."

"Why?" Holt demanded. "I'm one gun." He glanced at Sam. "Or two."

"That's part of it," Fool's Eagle said. "You two are also witnesses."

"I don't understand," Sam said.

"I do," Holt said in a hard voice. "You want us to lead you in a war against Quint, so it doesn't look entirely like some latter-day massacre of whites by Indians. We're supposed to be your dogsbodies, lend the whole business ... what's the word?"

"Legitimacy," Sam said.

"You're partly correct," Fool's Eagle said. "We do need you, and Morgan as well. He is no fighter. His brother is useless and suspect in his loyalties, and his niece reckless. You must take charge."

"And do what?" Holt snapped. "Wait until all the wolfers have gathered in Lobo, and then ride in and gun them down?"

"That's one possibility," Pete Matt said mildly, "but we lose if we win."

"A lot of lives could be lost," Sam said. "On both sides."

"It's more than that," Pete Matt said. "We are redskins. Quint, for all his viciousness and inhumanity, is white. Even if we defeat him—kill him, in the extreme case—we will be blamed as the aggressors and hounded by the authorities into a far worse defeat."

"We must press him," Fool's Eagle urged, "force his hand now."

"What do you mean 'we'?"

Fool's Eagle rose, waded to stand before Holt. If he suffered any embarrassment with regard to Sam, he gave no sign. "For our part, we will help you get Gutt."

"Wonderful," Holt said. "What makes you certain that he'll even be around? You said yourself that he can't risk trying to take us for the reward. Right now, while Quint is returning from Fort Benton, Gutt could be heading for parts unknown."

"I also told you Quint has a yellow streak. He'll make it worthwhile for Gutt to see this out."

The sulfurous stench of the water made it suddenly hard to breathe, or so it seemed to Holt. "This whole business is a ball of maybes."

"Which is about all we have to work with." Fool's Eagle climbed from the pool and began to dress. "You are already committed. You know it, Sam knows it, and I know it."

"What I know," Sam said, "is that I'd better get some sleep."

She stood as well, and Holt looked quickly away, but not before he caught a glimpse of her, hourglass-shaped and white in the shifting steam. It took every ounce of whatever willpower remained to him to keep his eyes averted.

Which meant he was staring at Pete Matt, who in turn was feasting his gaze on Sam. "You take the tent next to mine," the chief called to her.

"Thank you," Sam said behind Holt.

Pete Matt lowered his voice. "You, too," he said to Holt. He smiled. "I think she cottons to you."

Chapter Seventeen

If there was one ray of humor in this grim business, it came from the expression on Stanley Morgan's face. Fool's Eagle had predicted correctly: no question that the rancher was surprised.

Morgan stood before his cabin, arms akimbo and mouth agape, while Charity, at his flank, took satisfaction in this scene. Holt touched two fingers to his hat brim and said, "Afternoon, Mr. Morgan." He gestured with a thumb over his shoulder. "I brought some visitors."

Holt turned in the saddle to follow Morgan's gaze. The Blackfeet were spread out behind him, Fool's Eagle and Sam amidst them. Most of the Indian men rode horses, while the women and children walked. Travois, transports of blankets spread between two tepee poles attached to the horses' saddles, held folded tents, bundles of clothing, provisions, and the rest of the Blackfeet worldly goods. Bringing up the rear was the gift cow that had been spared slaughter the previous night.

Those tribal members afoot had slowed them somewhat, but they'd set out not long after sunup. It was still two hours from rising, though, when the bustle of activity awakened Holt in the tent that he shared chastely and uncomfortably with Sam. When he dressed and came out, Holt saw that camp had been struck; this tepee was the only one left standing. Indeed, as soon as Sam emerged, a small army of women descended, and within minutes the tent was reduced to a bundle of poles and a folded square of cloth. By full daylight Holt and his adopted band were miles south of the hot spring and into Morgan's range. Now, Holt reckoned it was no later than about two o'clock.

Where he stood before the cabin, Morgan asked, "What goes on?"

Pete Matt rode up next to Holt, dismounted, bowed his head politely to Morgan. "My people appreciate your hospitality."

Morgan had the courtesy to offer his hand, but while he and Pete Matt shook, Morgan shot Holt an inquisitive glance.

"I'll explain," Holt said. "For now, where do you want them to set up camp? The closer to the house, the better."

Prospect Morgan emerged from the cabin. He wore no jacket, only coveralls bibbed up over his union suit, and he was unshaven and splotchy-complected. He rubbed bleary eyes with his knuckles, as if he been roused from a nap, or more likely a day-drinking-driven stupor.

Holt dismounted. Prospect's expression darkened as his sodden brain began to decipher what he was seeing, like a gathering storm a few moments before it erupted in a downpour.

Or in Prospect's case, some exceedingly stupid comment.

As Holt passed Morgan, the rancher released Pete Matt's hand and, making the best of the situation, said, "You are welcome here."

Prospect opened his mouth and Holt clamped a hand over it. That stifled his words but not his stench; he smelled like he'd bathed in a river of whiskey. His knees were rubbery as Holt marched him around the side of the cabin.

Holt propped him against the wall. Prospect tried to focus on him. "Where the hell do you get off?" Prospect said thickly.

"Go sleep it off in the bunkhouse," Holt suggested.

"You can't tell me."

Holt had no time for this foofaraw. He drew his gun.

"Figure on shooting me?" Prospect inquired, gulped greenly and dropped without warning to his knees.

Holt danced back, the spew of vomit just missing his

boots. Prospect coughed, spit, grunted, and then rolled onto his back in the dirty snow and immediately was breathing deeply and regularly.

"Guess not," Holt said, reholstering the weapon. He couldn't leave him out here, but he sure as hell wished to keep his distance. In the end, he dragged him by the ankles across the yard, Prospect's arms flopping and leaving a wake in the snow. Blackfeet women hid their faces behind palms and tittered.

Holt kicked open the bunkhouse door and dumped Prospect on the other side of the sill, but it was near as cold inside as out. He muttered another curse word and went to work on a fire.

It took him five minutes or so to get it blazing, freeing him to leave. By then, he saw when he stepped outside, several tepees were already pitched, bunched tight together upwind of the corrals, like a barbican buffering Morgan's headquarters from Lobo and Quint and the wolfers, Holt's bane, lurking off to the west.

Inside Morgan's cabin, Holt found something like a war council in session. The rancher sat at the table with Sam, Charity, Fool's Eagle, and Pete Matt. That accounted for all the chairs, so Holt took up by the stove. He was grateful for its warmth anyway; the day, or intimations of impending trouble, had given him a chill.

"It's a long shot," Morgan was saying, "but I can see the sense of it, and besides, I haven't much choice."

"Quint's prejudices blinded him," Fool's Eagle opined. "He'd never consider the possibility of us allying with you—or vice versa."

"Emma should have," Charity said.

Sam shook her head. "Not necessarily. I think there's a possibility they will be truly taken aback."

A bottle of whiskey sat in the table's middle, but only Sam and Morgan were partaking. Charity fidgeted.

Holt drew his pouch from his shirt pocket. "I will roll

the smokes," he offered, "if someone will fill me in on what the hell we are talking about."

No one spoke until Sam said, "Quint has gotten in touch with Pert."

Holt fumbled the cigarette he was rolling, scattering tobacco to the floor. "Where was he?"

"The question is where *is* he," Sam said. "The answer is Lobo, right this minute."

Holt gaped. "How do you know?"

"I went back to town this morning," Charity said. "I didn't show myself, but I saw him."

Holt held out a hand at shoulder level. "Dapper hombre about this high, likely dressed nice?"

Charity nodded. No one spoke while Holt took a second shot at making a smoke, succeeded, and presented it to Pete Matt, who said thanks. "I don't see how Pert could have turned up so quickly. What about Gutt?"

"He's there as well, along with most of the wolfers, and stragglers are still drifting in." Charity chewed on something. "How smart is he?"

"Savvier than average," Holt said. "This gigantism disease he suffers hasn't affected his mind."

"Then I'd imagine you've lost him for now," Charity said. "He has no reason to stay, and every reason in the world to run."

"Me, too," Holt pointed out.

"That's been discussed and settled," Sam said pointedly.

Holt was goddamn fed up with being pushed hither and yon. He stalked to the door, threw it open, stood in its frame and did not go farther.

After what seemed a long time Sam said, "You're letting the cold in."

Holt slammed the door more roughly than necessary. "What's Quint's next move?" he demanded.

"He is holding all the trump cards," Morgan said. " 'Or gives direct information,' " he quoted.

"Talk sense," Holt barked.

"To win the reward on you," Morgan explained, "Quint

needs only lead this Pert to you, which he will. The marshal will ride you off, and we will be at Quint's mercy." He gestured to take in Fool's Eagle and Pete Matt. "All of us."

Holt gazed from one face to the next, landing last on Sam. The expression she returned was blank, as if to say it was all up to him.

It wasn't, and Holt knew it. "So we wait," he said with resignation.

Pete Matt blew out smoke. "Guess so," the chief said, as calm as if they were discussing the weather's latest turn.

Chapter Eighteen

Sleep was the principal item in Holt's debit column, and he spent most of the afternoon making up for its lack. He awoke for supper feeling refreshed, ate with Sam and the Morgans in the cabin, and found himself yawning before the meal was finished. After going over guard duty assignments, he excused himself and returned to the bunkhouse and his cot's comfort.

Sam came to gently shake him awake around five in the morning. More snow had begun to fall during the night. The Indians' tents were blanketed with its whiteness, and the cows in the pens steamed faintly as body heat melted the flakes when they hit. The darkness gave the world a particularly frigid feeling, and Holt clutched the buffalo robe close as he paced the barnyard.

His watch was the last; the other shifts had been taken by Sam, Fool's Eagle, and Pretty On Top, who had ended his rebellion by riding in with the other Blackfeet renegade around sunset. Pete Matt chastised them, then accepted their contrition.

Holt stomped his feet to keep the blood circulating, buried his hands within the robe's folds. Still he was cold, and his weariness was not entirely gone. Several times during the night he'd awakened and gone outside to satisfy himself that all remained serene.

He reached the shadow of the bunkhouse, spun on his heel to continue his trek. Behind him a familiar voice said, "Hold right there, son."

Holt sighed deeply and kept his hands visible as he turned. "Top of the morning, Marshal Pert," he said.

He turned slowly. Pert held a gun, of course, but there was no tension to the moment. The marshal lounged back against the bunkhouse wall, one ankle crossed over the other, and his revolver was pointed at the ground between them.

"That was a nasty trick," Pert said. "It's lucky for you I am a good sport."

"Beg pardon?" Holt said.

"That bit of foolery down in Utah." Pert shook his head at the recollection. "I had the galloping trots for three days."

Holt had to smile. In the course of his pursuit for their supposed crimes, Pert had put them under arrest in a town called Provo, and was preparing to take them in when he succumbed to a weakness for chili con carne. Unfortunately for Pert, his bowl was laced with a powerful purgative, and while he was answering nature's urgent call, Holt and Sam made their escape.

"Wipe that smirk off your face, young fellow," Pert said.

"Sorry, Marshal. No permanent ill effects, I hope."

"One, actually. I lost my taste for chili." Pert straightened. "You got a gun under all that hair you're wearing?"

"Sure."

"Give it over."

Holt dug out his revolver and handed it to the marshal, holding it by the barrel.

"Your horse up in the barn?" Pert said. Holt nodded, and Pert said, "Saddle up."

Holt peered at him through the snow and put his finger on what was wrong here: Pert had shown no interest in rousting out Sam.

"Where are we going?" Holt asked.

Pert stowed Holt's weapon in his belt. "We are going," he said, "to give you a chance to save your life."

* * *

Holt thought that he wouldn't mind being hale as Pert when he reached the marshal's age—*if*, he mentally amended.

Pert was somewhere in his fifties, but sat his horse with the erectness of a man two decades younger, with no signs of the aches and pains of middle years. He was dressed lightly for the weather in a buckskin jacket, clean white shirt, four-in-hand tie, and serge slacks, but he evinced no discomfort. He rode at Holt's side, having put away his weapon before mounting up. Though no discussion had taken place, Holt understood he was a tacit partner in an agreement that he would not act up.

Though they rode west in the direction of Lobo, something told him that was not their destination. He didn't bother to try to ferret out what was going on; he'd spent a good twenty-four hours with the marshal in Utah, long enough to learn something of his odd ways.

"How did you get here so quickly?"

"I am dogged," Pert said automatically.

"I recollect you telling me that, more than once," Holt said. It was the marshal's catch phrase.

"As you are determined to find and confront this Gutt," Pert said, "I have been determined to find you and Miss Lowell. And like Gutt, you and she stand out from the ordinary citizenry and cause tongues to wag." Pert considered Holt critically. "This business of changing your hair and all won't work."

"Not anymore," Holt muttered.

"I am determined to see justice done," Pert went on in his preoccupied way.

"Then you have the wrong fellow."

Pert surprised Holt once again. "There exists that possibility, son. Incidentally, Fitzsimmons won."

"Stringer is dead?"

In Utah, Holt had had the chance to give Pert his version of how one of the two men was behind his being framed for the murder of Cat Lacey, as an expedient if vicious way of getting him out of the picture.

"Probably not," Pert answered. "Fitzsimmons's mines should have played out, but they haven't yet. Ultimately he became wealthy enough to buy Stringer out."

Holt chewed on this new piece of information. "How do you know all this?"

At their backs the first faint glow of dirty dawn colored the horizon, and in its meager illumination Holt made out the tree line that marked the course of the milky river.

"A federal officer is not like another man," Pert said.

"True in your case," Holt muttered.

Pert glanced at him. "I'll take that as a compliment, son. What I meant is that I am trained to be dispassionate. I cannot hold a grudge."

"Are we back to that bowl of chili?"

"I believe your story," Pert said.

"That's nice," Holt said, utterly at sea as to where this discourse was heading.

"I pretty much believed it when I heard it in Utah," Pert continued. "I was swayed by the way you put your own freedom in peril to help those Jewish folks down there. I went to Argentville, where I learned that Stringer pulled up stakes."

The milky river was a hundred yards distant. Pert reined up. "I operated under cover of a traveling drummer. I was quite convincing."

"No doubt."

"In that guise, I was able to talk to people, from which I further developed my opinion that you are innocent."

Holt wasn't yet ready to indulge in a sense of relief. "So you no longer mean to bring us in?"

"Of course I do," Pert said complacently. "I am dogged."

"Jeez Louise," Holt exploded. "What the hell are you yabbering about?"

Pert thumped his horse and they rode on. "You will face a court of law for retrial, this time with Gutt as your witness. But first I must be sure in my own mind."

Holt drew a deep breath. "Just out of curiosity," he said,

wrestling to keep his tone patient, "what would convince you?"

"His answers and his demeanor," Pert said, "when you confront him."

Holt felt a chill not due to the wintry season. "Where and when is this confrontation to take place?"

Pert pointed ahead. Holt peered through the snow and made out the flicker of flame at the base of one of the aspens by the river. At the edge of its light, a squat bulk hunkered.

"Over there," Pert answered, "and right now."

Gutt was a sight to see, and hardly a welcome one. He was not an easy man to lay eyes on, let alone subdue. "How'd you do it?" Holt asked Pert.

"I snuck up on him while he slept," the marshal said, "put a gun to his temple and announced he was under arrest as a material witness to murder."

"You've got a lot of crust," Holt said, with frank admiration.

Gutt stared up at them with an effect that Holt found distinctly disconcerting. Some of the people of the Utah town called Golem, near where Holt had his prior confrontation with the big man, believed him to be a spirit, a monster born of their worst dreams. Though not superstitious, Holt could see how a person might embrace such a notion.

Even seated as he was, with his wrists manacled behind him so his arms were drawn around the tree's trunk, Gutt was the picture of menace. Erect he stood nearly seven feet tall, and his disorder made him monstrous beyond his size. His eyes were sunk deeply in bony sockets capped with exaggerated ridged brows, and his mottled face was nearly square-shaped. His long dark hair, made lank by the melted snow that wetted it, hung to his shoulders. Everything about his countenance was knotty, from the cheekbones that bulged and twitched beneath his facial skin to the gnarled knuckles of his hands. Although he sat at ease with his head lolled to one side, his presence bristled with energy, poised to burst into violence the moment it was unleashed.

"I was far from sanguine," Pert said. "I expected at any moment he would turn, and introduce me to my Maker."

"Maybe you ought to have a gun in hand now," Holt suggested. "Just in case."

"Goes against my grain," Pert said, "seeing as how he is incapacitated already."

"What now?" Holt felt Gutt's stare as if it radiated heat. "Begin your interview. Compel him to convince me."

Gutt cleared his throat. "Don't speak of me as if I were not here." His voice was guttural in tone but not uncultured in his choice of words; he'd had some learning, he'd told Holt in their other meeting. "The Morgan girl," he said. "She tell you I saved her from bothersome doings?"

"Yes."

"I've been working to hone my social graces." Gutt's laughter sounded like a sack of chains dragged over gravel. "Seriously, I thought I'd try going straight, but as through all my life, people won't let me be, and besides, there is slim profit in the straight life for one such as me."

Holt felt uncomforting premonitions; they came with the territory when Gutt was a part of it. Holt saw mixed emotions as well in Pert's expression: revulsion, a touch of pity, more than a little apprehension.

"Also," Gutt said to Holt, "I knew that despite my warning, you were still after me. That's why I'm here now." He turned his gaze to Pert. "I let you get the drop on me, Marshal."

"Sure you did," Pert said, "and now stories are waiting to be told."

"Not this morning," Gutt said, and did magic.

Pert drew his gun as Gutt stood, but it was too late to bring it all the way up. The aspen came with him; Holt would wonder ever after how any man could have the strength to uproot a tree that was thirty feet tall and eighteen inches across at the base.

But wonderment would have to wait. Gutt, his arms still

linked behind him, made a gesture like a bow. The tree descended in tandem, cracking Pert smartly on the head. The marshal went down without a whimper.

Holt danced back out of the falling branches' range. The tree shuddered and fell away from Gutt. The big man did something awkward that Holt could not clearly see through the snow and dim dawn and his dismay, then pushed the tree trunk aside and came into view with his manacled hands now in front of him.

Holt took two more steps backward, reached automatically for his gun, remembered it was in the marshal's belt.

Gutt stood between him and Pert's inert form, no more than ten yards distant. "What did I tell you in Utah?"

They both knew the answer to that one, nor did Gutt expect a reply.

"I told you I am brutal by nature," Gutt reminded him. As if in confirmation, he bent to Pert, and Holt thought he meant to break the marshal's neck. To his relief, Gutt only rifled Pert's pockets until he found the key to the manacles.

"I told you I would kill you if you persisted in harassing me." Gutt unlocked one cuff, then the other. "Now I shall." He ignored the guns, as if they played no role in what he had in mind.

Gutt advanced on Holt.

Running like hell made plenty of sense, but there was Doakes—and what in hell did the bushwhacker who Sam shot two days earlier have to do with this? Holt understood: maybe that incident had to do with fear or maybe not, but fleeing now sure as hell would decide the issue, and—

Gutt was upon him, grabbed at Holt's shoulders and rode him down into the snow. His bulk pressed the breath from Holt's lungs.

Gutt clasped his huge hands around Holt's neck.

Time was suspended. Holt's world stood still, pending the slightest flex of Gutt's grip. All was tableau, an existence eclipsed by the craggy visage hovering a few inches before Holt's eyes.

"I killed her." Gutt's voice was guttural, and his breath in

Holt's face was rich and swampy. "That is the admission you wish to hear from me before you die."

"Don't," Holt gasped.

Gutt's expression became a parody of a smile. "You are a coward." His spittle flecked Holt's cheek. "You are yellow as Kansas corn in August."

Of all the thoughts that might have passed his mind in what could be his last moments of animation, the one that came was: *No. I may be many things, but that is not one of them.*

Time passed, Gutt's face nose to nose with Holt's. After a while his hands lowered, to grab Holt at either side. Gutt rose, taking Holt with him as if he weighed no more than a straw-stuffed scarecrow.

Gutt whirled in a full circle and let Holt go. He flew through the air, flailing like a cat trying to land on its feet. He floundered and hit hard on his back instead.

Gutt followed.

Holt scrambled up, feinted to his left, and as Gutt went with the move, Holt raced toward Pert. He dove over the marshal's form, got both hands on the gun lying beside him, rolled and brought it up.

Gutt towered over him. "To me this is sport."

Holt waved the gun. "Don't move again."

Gutt barely acknowledged the weapon. "You and I are bound up together," he said. "You can't do me harm."

"Bet your life I can," Holt suggested.

Gutt shook his head. "You won't kill because you need me alive. You won't plink me in the leg or some such because you don't have the grit." Gutt studied him. "Maybe you do," he decided, "but it wouldn't suit your purpose."

Gutt stepped back. Holt got to his feet, his finger on the trigger.

"I scared you in Utah," Gutt said.

"You scared me plenty."

"Not enough to stop you from following me again." Gutt stared off into the gathering dawn. "I took you for craven, but it appears I was wrong."

He looked at Holt. "I reckon this is going to be another inconclusive interview," he decided.

Gutt turned his back on Holt. It made a massive target, and Holt lined his gun on it.

And saw that Gutt was right twice. Holt did need him alive; and fright and cowardice were different kettles of fish.

"Gutt!" Holt called.

The big man stopped near the line of trees.

Holt lowered his weapon. "Why didn't you strangle me when you had the chance?"

Over his shoulder, Gutt gave Holt a hideous grin. "Like I said, we're bound up. That's not to say I won't do it, next time you give me the opportunity."

Gutt moved on, and the curtain of darkness and snow swallowed him up.

Holt took a step after him—and to what purpose? He replaced the gun where it belonged and went to Pert.

The marshal had not moved. Holt bent to tend to him, hoping his skull wasn't cracked. The last thing he needed on his hands was a dead lawman.

Holt soaked his neckerchief in the creek and held the cloth cupped in his hands. He splashed what collected in Pert's face and wrung out the bandanna on him as well. In the thirty seconds or so that took, Holt's hands turned splotchy from the icy water. He wiped them on his coat and rubbed them together until normal color returned.

By then Pert was stirring. "Better dry yourself," Holt said, "before your nose freezes off."

Pert sat up and did as he was told. "You are a jinx, son." His voice was a little shaky, but he seemed mostly all right. "Every time I hook up with you, someone makes a monkey of me."

"If you don't get your butt off the ground, you'll be a frozen money."

Holt helped Pert to his feet. "Thanks," Pert said.

"You seeing double or anything like that?"

"I hurt, but I will live. I am a tough old bird."

About ten minutes had elapsed since Gutt's disappearance, and although Holt didn't expect he'd lurk around these parts, or even this territory now that he'd gotten free, Holt went cautiously as he followed Gutt's tracks. The snowfall was rapidly filling them in, and after about fifty yards they turned into the tree cover along the stream and disappeared altogether.

"Queer fellow, that Gutt," Pert said as Holt returned. "Got the drop on you as well, I suppose."

Holt didn't much feel like going into details.

"Did he steal a horse?" Pert went on.

"No."

Pert put away his handkerchief. "Likely didn't want to be robbing a U.S. Marshal."

"Probably reckoned that you're dogged."

"You're joshing again, son."

Holt shook his head impatiently. "If you're good enough to ride, let's get the hell back to the ranch."

Pert hesitated. "I'm thinking I should return to town to make certain Quint knows of my continued presence."

"And give me the chance to run out on you?"

Pert regarded him. "You're not going anywhere until this Quint business is settled."

"What do you know about it?"

"Pretty much the whole story, I'd warrant. I had already tracked you far as Fort Benton, and I did some interviewing there before Quint found me. He is quite the topic of conversation in this section of the territory."

Holt tried to roll a cigarette, but with his hands exposed he could not keep them dry of melting snow, and the paper turned soggy and tore. "I'd stay away from Quint for the moment," he said. "He'll come to you."

"How do you figure that?"

Holt gestured to indicate the storm. "Even one dogged as you would not attempt any long-distance riding in this weather, and the only other shelter besides Lobo is Morgan's place. Quint'll know we're holed up there."

Pert looked uncomfortable. "That is exactly the problem," he said. "If I read Quint right, he is not the sort to give up eight thousand dollars in reward money. But to collect, he needs to be with me when I find you."

Holt snorted in exasperation. "You already found me."

"Quint doesn't know that. If I can get back quick enough, he never will. I'll return with him, pretend to follow his scouting, and—"

"Wait a Texas minute," Holt exploded. "You're going to sell me out to a son of a bitch like Quint?"

Pert was abashed. "You are to be taken into my custody anyway."

"I thought you said you believed my story."

"What I believe is neither here nor there. I am but the law's handmaiden. You must hope that a jury believes you." Pert looked grave. "I will testify to your character, however."

"Wonderful. I really appreciate that."

"Sarcasm ill suits you, son. I must do what I must do." He cleared his throat. "Right now that is to return to Lobo before Quint discovers my absence."

"Shut up," Holt said.

For a moment Pert took the order as escalation in the debate, and was about to speak when he stopped himself. He heard it, too.

From somewhere to the east came the snort of horses and their muffled tread, along with men's voices. The damping effect of the snow's curtain made it hard to estimate distance, but they were close and moving closer.

"I'd say Quint has made his discovery," Holt whispered.

"Doubtless he is not pleased."

"Good guess," Holt hissed. "Now let's ride."

Chapter Nineteen

Holt swung out of the saddle before the bay came to a complete stop. It snorted great blasts of steam and its belly heaved with exertion. Pert's horse was equally ill-used, and Holt was concerned for both animals. He and the marshal had driven them to near-full gallop from the milky river, to cover the few miles back to the ranch in less than a half hour, while the day brightened from gray to dingy, snow-filled white. But even that short a distance took its toll in this sort of cold, and both horses were soaked with snow-melt and their own froth.

Holt was about to holler for Charity when Pete Matt and Fool's Eagle hove into view from the direction of their encampment. Pete Matt sized up the urgency of the situation, clapped his hands and called out something in his language. Several women materialized and took the horses' reins. "They'll be rubbed down and grained," Pete Matt said. He ran a brown hand over the bay's flank as it passed. "They'll survive."

"Let's hope the same goes for us," Holt said. "I need warmth and coffee and Morgan. We've got maybe fifteen minutes to get our details straight."

In the cabin, Charity had set out a fresh pot at the sound of their arrival. Sam looked up from where she sat at the table. "Good morning, Marshal Pert," she said. "Long time no see."

Across from her, Morgan appraised Holt. "It's come to the showdown."

"That's right." Pert had returned Holt's handgun, and as

165

he filled them in he checked the cylinder, then wiped the weapon down. As he finished the story, he realized the party was one hombre short. "Where's Prospect?"

"Gone," Morgan said. "Likely turned yellow and run."

Holt pondered on that while Charity fetched him a cup of coffee. He thanked her and sent her to the bunkhouse to fetch his and Sam's rifles.

"First off," he continued to Pete Matt, "get your women and children into the barn. There's a drop bar, and they'll—"

Pete Matt shook his head. "They'll not be shut up like livestock," he said.

"I didn't mean to suggest that. It's for their own safety."

"And terror. They will hear the fight and think of their men, and they will panic in the darkness. And if we are defeated—"

"There will be no battle royale," Pert declared. "The law will not permit it."

Holt whirled on him, slopping coffee on his hand. "You're living in a dreamworld, Pert," he snapped. "The way things have turned out, you now stand between Quint and everything he wants—the reward on us, Morgan's property, control of this territory."

"He will not prevail."

"He will with you out of the way," Holt insisted. "I'll bet you bullion to bullets he's given orders that you are to be the first to go down. A stray slug from someone in the snow's cover, no one to say who fired it—maybe there are times when even a desperado will hesitate to kill a lawman, but this is not one of them."

Pert paled and rubbed at his aching forehead. "Still I must do my duty."

"You do what you want." Holt turned to the others. "The rest of us already decided what we've got to do." They'd argued out their course and refined it the previous evening.

WINTER OF THE WOLF 167

Charity threw back the door and entered with the long guns. "It's time," she said, breathing hard.

Holt strained his ears, and to them came the sound of the approaching riders.

As Holt reached the far side of the corral, he saw a dozen or more men sitting their horses, ghostly behind the snow's screen and maybe fifty feet away. Behind him Blackfoot warriors slipped between the pens.

Sam came up and whispered, "You ready?"

Holt squared his shoulders, hollered, "You men!"

For a long beat he got only silence in response. Then one of them called, "Is that you, Holt?" The voice was vaguely familiar, but not Quint's. "I hope so," it went on. "Aside from the general business of the morning, you and me got a personal score to settle."

"Quint misinformed you," Holt shouted. "You are trespassing, and there are twenty rifles trained on you and ready to enforce Morgan's rights."

Two of the figures moved forward. Holt took a few steps to meet them, the rifle aimed at the ground but ready, and Sam at his back covering him.

The figures resolved into clearer view, and Holt gaped at them. Both were done up like the phony Indians he'd seen two mornings earlier on the milky river, in buckskins, blankets, and with lank hair done in braids and stained dark with boot black. Quint must have gone a little demented in his anger at Pert's apparent betrayal, Holt thought, along with his lust to capture him and drive off Morgan; apparently this was a feeble attempt to throw the marshal off track, though it did have the minor advantage of providing the wolfers with some anonymity to cover the murders they no doubt had come to commit.

"I don't see but two rifles," one of the men said as they rode up. He peered past Holt. "I'll be dragged and dipped," he exclaimed. "I got both of you, the bitch that shot me and you," he said to Holt, "the one who stomped me."

That made him Farley, sided by his apple-headed partner Moon. "You're way outnumbered," Holt said.

"You're full of crap." Farley pointed a finger at Sam. "And you are dead meat." He stroked absently at his thigh. "Still hurts when the weather turns this cold."

"Tell them to disarm," Holt ordered.

"When cows grow wings," Farley snapped, and reached for his sidearm.

Holt fired first, into the air. Before Farley could clear leather, the dim snow-choked morning erupted in gunfire.

The volley came from either side, twenty shots fired nearly simultaneously. None hit a target and none was meant to, the slugs passing harmless over the heads of the band of men. "That's how full of crap I am," Holt said to Farley.

The men behind the big wolfer—Holt saw now that they were all duded up like he, as ersatz Indians—milled dangerously. "The next salvo will be aimed lower," he hollered to them.

They had weapons in hand, looked around nervously for targets. But Pete Matt's Blackfeet warriors had slipped back out of sight into the snowfall's cover.

"Dismount," Holt ordered. "Guns to the ground and hands to the sky." To Farley he said, "You first. Set a good example."

Farley shook his head. "You're bluffing. Them Injuns ain't about to slaughter white men."

"I might," Sam said. "You threatened me."

Farley still had his hand on his holstered revolver, and regarded her with faint amusement. This was playing out too long, Holt thought, and felt control of the tense standoff slipping through his fingers.

"You should have plugged me good and proper, 'stead of plinking me in the leg," Farley said to Sam. "Now it's my turn."

He pulled his pistol.

Sam gasped and shot him out of the saddle. Before he hit

the ground, Holt said, "Aw hell," because the shot would be taken as another signal, and—

"Hold fire," Holt screamed.

It was too late. Before the two words were all the way out, another thunderous volley cut loose.

Holt froze—but no one else moved either, nor was hit. Holt blew out breath in vast relief. Someone had countermanded Holt's orders, and a damned good thing it was.

Better yet, it worked. Holt heard a wolfer say, "Farley's dead. It ain't much loss, but I don't mean to be next." He dismounted, lay a rifle in the snow and a revolver beside it, and raised his hands, moving carefully toward Holt.

Already others were following suit, and the capitulation became general. Holt wanted to convince himself that this just might work after all, except that one element—one very bothersome element—was missing.

As if to confirm his apprehension, another shot was fired.

The advancing men paused, but the report was at some distance. Keep the momentum, the upper hand, Holt admonished himself. One step at a time.

"Morgan!" he called.

The rancher appeared along with Charity; the two had been covering the action from in front of the cabin, though if Holt's plan hadn't worked, they would have been goners. Morgan herded the disarmed wolfers into one of the pens. The cattle shied back at this influx of humans. Morgan ordered them to stay huddled closely and took a position where he could guard against insurrection.

"Them cows stink worse than us," someone muttered.

"It'll keep your mind off mischief," Holt snapped.

Farley's partner Moon had not moved since Sam dropped Farley. His round face was pale and blank, as if in his mind he had gone away from there. Holt went up to him and carefully took the rifle from his hands, then shook him by the leg. "Snap out of it," Holt said. "Where is Quint?" And who the hell shot whom a minute earlier? Holt wondered, pretty sure the two questions were connected.

Moon turned his expressionless gaze on Holt. "He said it'd be better if Farley was the leader." Moon looked at his partner. "But now that gal kilt him."

"Climb down," Holt ordered.

As Moon complied, his face reanimated. "Farley!" Moon cried.

Holt spun. Farley was not dead after all, but neither was he a threat. When he sat up, his gun arm hung crooked and limp, and the movement brought a quick spurt of blood that dribbled down the right side of his blanket. "My shoulder is shattered into a million bits," he said, "and I think I'm fixing to bleed to death."

"You will," Holt said, "if you don't tell me Quint's whereabouts."

Moon crouched beside Farley and produced a dirty bandanna from somewhere. He pressed it against the bullet wound, the seepage slowing while the cloth reddened. "Best for all if we did this job," Moon said to Holt.

"Shut up," Farley snapped.

"We're all gonna get two hundred, and that's on top of what we make when this is done and we go back to the mountains." Moon wiped fever sweat from Farley's forehead with an absent sweep of the back of his hand. "Quint said."

"Put a sock in it, you little pissant." But this time Farley was not to strike his partner. Vehemence used up the last of his strength, and he passed out.

Fool's Eagle said, "Let's finish up."

Holt turned. Fool's Eagle stood with Pete Matt to one side; Holt had no way of knowing how long they'd been there. "Doesn't look like we're going to finish," Holt muttered. "Not today."

He felt antsy and disgruntled, unresolved despite the partial success, but he must push on. "Can you spare a couple of men to watch him?" Holt asked Pete Matt.

The chief nodded. To Moon, Holt said, "Get Farley into that bunkhouse yonder, build a fire, and see to him. Don't put much truck in Blackfeet not killing white men. Farley

WINTER OF THE WOLF 171

could die yet, and you will for sure if you try any wrong moves."

Pete Matt finished speaking in his language, as two of his men materialized to help Moon wrestle Farley up. The pain of it brought him partially around, and he moaned pitifully as he was toted off. Holt was pleased to see that this produced some thoughtful looks among the penned wolfers. He was beginning to recognize their type: men worthless for much beyond mayhem, and convinced that they were immune from its results—until someone else's mortality got rubbed in their faces.

"I will take over now." Pert appeared at Holt's elbow.

"Where the hell have you been?"

"With the Blackfeet," Pert said, "making sure none of them decided on his own to gun anyone."

"So it was you that changed the plan?"

"And a good thing," Pert said. "Imagine my awkward situation if killery had occurred and I must explain my part in it." Pert placed a hand on Holt's shoulder. "You did good, son, and contrary to what you said, this is finished after all. I have these hombres dead to rights."

Pert stalked to the corral, faced the men within. "Listen up," he announced. "I am U.S. Federal Marshal Clennon T. Pert."

"What's the T stand for?" someone muttered.

"No sass," Pert admonished. "You are under arrest, every man of you."

"Oh for Christ's sake," Holt muttered. "We've got other fish to fry."

Pert ignored him, readdressed himself to the wolfers. They looked fairly pathetic, Holt thought sourly, disarmed and done up in their wild-west-show redskin costumes.

Sam touched at his arm. "What about Quint?"

"What about him?" Holt said sourly.

At the corral, Pert was into what for all the world seemed like a formal oration. "You have been led astray by this Quint. He has inveigled you into riding on innocent citizens with violent intent. This is contrary to the law, and I am its handmaiden."

"That sounds familiar," Holt muttered.

"In addition," Pert went on, "you intended to take from me my prisoner. This troubles me, but though I am dogged, I can see expediency when I must."

"The hell is he talking about?" Holt whispered to Sam.

"I am confiscating your weapons," Pert said. Indeed, several Blackfoot women were finishing the chore of gathering up the guns the wolfers had dropped. "You may keep your horses, and you will use them to depart from these precincts," Pert said. "Pickings would have been slim this season in any case."

Pert looked over his shoulder at Holt. "This wolfing has been in progress for a half-dozen years. The poor beastie is nearly wiped out. Now is the time for Mr. Morgan to accept that there are worse predators than lobos."

Morgan regarded Pert with a mixture of admiration and abashment. He nodded slowly.

"Unpen them," Pert said. "I will remain for some days, and if I encounter any one of you past tomorrow, you will answer to justice."

This was a bit too unreal for Holt's tastes. He stepped forward, poked at Pert with his forefinger. "You think we might learn a bit more about Quint's whereabouts before you set these thugs free?"

Pert frowned. "Good point, son. Where do you suppose he is?"

Across the yard by the barn, someone said, "I'll ask the questions."

Holt peered through the snow, his revolver in hand. It was Quint, all right—Holt could make out the steel plate's reflection—but it was not he who had spoken. He sat his horse motionlessly, and held no gun.

"Climb down, Quint." Holt moved toward him. "Your men are disarmed, and there are plenty of weapons covering you."

WINTER OF THE WOLF 173

Quint dismounted without protest. As he came forward, he carefully opened his buffalo robe. Holt thumbed back the hammer of his Colt.

"You planning to commit murder?" Quint said. He showed Holt his empty holster.

"What goes on?"

"This and that." Another advanced on horseback. Holt saw the yellowed teeth between fat lips buried in a nest of matted beard that belonged to Geeson.

Pert pushed past Holt. "Mr. Quint," he declared. "You are under arrest for rustling and inciting to violence."

"To hell with that," Quint said. "You got nothing at all can connect me to this business, and no one will testify different." He raised his voice in the direction of the penned wolfers. "That's the truth and it'll stay the truth, unless anyone wants to answer to me."

Pert said to Holt in a low voice, "He is right, son. I guess we have failed to stop him."

Geeson climbed down from his horse. He was holding what was likely Quint's own gun on him, which explained one fraction of whatever the hell was going on, Holt thought.

Geeson's years in the mountains must have sharpened his hearing, for he said to Pert, in response, "Maybe not."

"What are you doing here?" Holt asked.

"I'll ask the questions." Geeson looked around elaborately. "Seems like the place to be. I wasn't about to take part in Quint's little costume party—hell, he didn't even invite me, so I guess I'm not the one who is going to tie him into this for you. But I'm curious as the next Joe, so I thought I'd mosey on down and see how this fandango turned out. I walked on out of the mountains, sort of borrowed a horse from Quint's livery, and here I am."

Geeson regarded Pert. "You the marshal I heard about?" He looked Pert up and down. "Dapper sort of fellow, aren't you. Who you after?"

Pert gaped at Geeson.

"He knows the story," Holt said resignedly. "Hell, there aren't but a few people here who don't."

Geeson nodded. "I figured so, when I heard Quint was fetching the law. That's another reason I happened by. I decided that I believed you—anyway, your story passed the time when you were my house guest—so I thought I'd see maybe could I further your case."

"Thanks." Holt cocked his head to indicate Pert. "But it looks like it's too late."

Geeson looked past Holt to where Sam and Charity were standing. "Which one of them is your woman?"

Sam stepped forward and told him her name. Holt said, "This here is Geeson."

"Ma'am," Geeson said politely.

And wasn't this all so nice and sociable, Holt thought bitterly. "Looks to me like this is wrapped up, but not neatly," he said to Pert. "Unless you got any more ideas."

"I got one, regarding Quint here," Geeson said.

Quint paled, said, "Watch your mouth, old man," but the force of conviction was lacking.

"Take your own advice," Geeson snapped. To Pert he said, "A few minutes ago I watched him gun down a man in cold blood. For some reason I decided not to mind my own business, so I got the drop on him with my rifle and made him give me this peashooter." He gestured with the revolver.

"Who was the victim?" Pert said.

"Fellow in his middle years who appeared to be no stranger to strong drink." Geeson regarded Morgan. "Looked like he could have been your kin."

Holt glanced back at Charity to find a stricken look on her face. "Whatever he was, he was my father," she snapped at him.

Oblivious to her grief, Geeson continued. "He come up to Quint, starts babbling about the Indians you got here and how you probably mean an ambush, goes on about the lawman and all. Quint waits until he finishes, then pops a hole in his tripes."

"Jesus," Holt said. "You can spare us the details."

Pert had brightened considerably. "And you will testify to such in a court of law?"

"Nope," Geeson said complacently.

"Damned straight," Quint snapped. "It'll be your word against mine, and mine will be that you did the deed."

"That's not it," Geeson said. "Everyone knows that I never owned a handgun in my life, and when they dig the slug out of the poor sucker, it'll be a Colt's .45 caliber shortie."

"You must do your duty as a citizen."

Geeson shook his head at Pert. "I'm fifty-seven years old, and feeling older. Could be Quint might beat the charge, and then he'd come gunning for me. I don't need the headache."

Pert grimaced in frustration. He dug out his handcuffs as he stepped up to Quint. "Nonetheless you are under arrest for suspicion. Present your wrists."

A rifle barked.

Pert's hat flew from his head, pirouetted in the air, and drifted to the ground. The marshal froze in place.

"You'll take the next one in the brains," the shootist called, "if everyone doesn't drop their weapons pronto."

The newcomer eased into view from Holt's left holding the rifle on Pert and dressed as the wolfers in Blackfeet costume, but with the face masked with a neckerchief. Holt lowered his revolver. Before he could let go of it, the intruder said, "Not you."

The voice was deep but affected, as if deliberately disguised. "Yours goes in the holster," it intoned. "You will need it."

"This is insane," Holt barked.

"And contrary to the law." Pert's words were strained and breathy, because the masked intruder held him around the neck in a choke hold. The other hand pressed a revolver to the base of Pert's skull, and he had been dragged off to the side so he was a shield against any potential gunfire, should someone get reckless.

In the midst of the barnyard, Holt and Quint stood facing each other at a distance of ten paces. The gun that Geeson had lifted from Quint was now back in its holster on the newcomer's order, and Quint's right hand hung suspended a few inches from its butt.

"This is a fair fight according to the law, Mr. Marshal." Pert winced as the gun jammed a little harder at the nape of his neck. "With fifty witnesses to see it is such."

"And my neck on the line," Quint muttered. It struck Holt that he was not completely surprised at the turn of events, nor hardly pleased.

"The only way to finish it. And you will not lose."

"You're sure of that," Quint said.

"He's yellower even than you. I know this."

Quint muttered, but under his breath said, "Button your trap."

"Gutt told me he was yellow. Gun him!"

Holt stared at Quint. "Gutt was deadly wrong—deadly for you."

Quint leaned forward on the balls of his feet, was poised there, his fingers twitching. Holt knew he must draw—if he did not, Pert would die, but if he did—

"I will see you all arrested," Pert announced. "I am dogged."

"Holy Joan on the pyre," Holt muttered—and in that fraction of a second his concentration was diverted.

Holt saw Quint's steel jaw beyond the snowfall, and the gun emerge from Quint's holster. His own hand was moving, but at the same time he was possessed by the scene of that morning, Gutt chasing him like a mouse harried by a cat, and him running. . . .

Holt drew and was way too late. Quint fired before Holt's gun cleared leather.

But Holt was moving, and miraculously, Quint missed. He tried to thumb back the hammer of his single-action revolver, and did manage to get it cocked, but all the while—

WINTER OF THE WOLF 177

and it seemed to take forever—his expression was that of a man condemned.

Holt held his gun up in both hands, hurrying his aim. He fired and saw sparks.

Quint stumbled backward and went down, but sat up immediately. He touched almost curiously at his steel jaw. A dimple had appeared in its center.

Quint recovered, tried for a second shot. Holt drilled him in the chest. Quint punched back, rolled over twice, astonishingly turned himself in Holt's direction and made ready to fire.

Holt shot him a third time, and then a fourth. Quint twitched massively, threw out his arm and released the gun, lay still.

Holt stumbled forward. Quint was on his back, blood oozing like lava from his heart. Holt thought he could hear the hiss as snow descended and melted as it hit the fallen wolfer boss.

Holt knelt, touched his finger to the side of Quint's neck. He knew he must be dead, but needed tangible confirmation, and also to get his head lower than his torso, because he felt a wave of nausea rising.

"Holt!" Sam hollered.

He roused himself, turned in time to see Pert fall to hands and knees, but no sign of whoever the hell had orchestrated this drama of bloody mayhem. Before Holt could figure out what was going on, Sam rushed past, stooped to retrieve her gun before she leaped upon Geeson's horse.

"Hey," Geeson said.

Quint's animal was shying from the commotion. Holt caught it by the bridle, jerked its head down to show who was in charge, managed to get aboard, and followed Sam a moment after she disappeared into the snowfall.

Sam disregarded his hollered orders to stop, and he lost her now and again in the storm. Holt swore, raked at the horse's flanks, galloped through the whiteness, but made no progress in catching up.

The light turned strange and the snow began to abate in the onslaught of one ray of sunshine, then stopped completely as the day suddenly lightened. Ahead Holt saw Sam, and no more than ten yards beyond, the stranger who had fled, now halted and turned and aiming at Sam.

Holt hollered again, and Sam charged on. The stranger spun away and fired a wild shot. Sam vaulted from the saddle. She gathered her feet beneath her and dove, driving her shoulder into the other's middle. They tumbled to the ground, rolled in the snow.

Holt reached them, pitched off the horse, fell to one knee, and righted himself in time to see Sam pound a fist into her antagonist's face.

Sam stood; the other did not move. Sam stepped back, breathing hard.

"That felt good when I did it." Sam massaged her knuckles. "But I think I hurt my hand."

"Remind me to teach you how to punch," Holt said, "and what the hell is this madcap chase about?"

"You didn't guess?"

Holt peered at the fallen figure. "Guess what?"

Sam bent, jerked away the neckerchief that covered the face, removed the hat. A dark wig came away with it.

Emma Frank shuddered, opened her eyes, and said, "You'd never have taken me in a fair fight."

Holt gaped at her. Sam stood, paced a few steps, turned and came back. She showed Holt her palm, tried to make a fist.

"I can't flex my middle finger," she said. "Is that a bad sign?"

Clennon Pert came up on foot. "So it was you behind all these shenanigans," he said.

Emma stood, but kept her hands in sight. "Someone must act as a man. I should have known it would not be Quint."

She stared at Holt with terrific fury, but of all possibilities, he would never have guessed that a moment later her gaze would lower as she began to sob. Holt felt almost embarrassed.

Not far away, someone moaned piteously. It gave Holt a reason to move from there, as Pert went to handcuff Emma.

Holt found Prospect Morgan a couple of dozen yards distant. Miraculously, he was not dead, though he was surely dying. He'd been gut-shot; Holt could smell the pungent scent of his punctured entrails, and saw he had little time left.

Holt thought Prospect recognized who he was. "Tell him," Prospect moaned.

"What?"

"I didn't hate him." Prospect meant his brother, Morgan. "I didn't want to betray him. But Quint offered—"

Holt wiped cold sweat from Prospect's forehead.

"—what I thought I deserved," Prospect got out. "My birthright, my fair share of my brother's success."

Holt started as Stanley Morgan said behind him, "If you had asked."

"Couldn't." Prospect focused on Holt. "There's yellow and there's yellow, and mine was plenty worse than Quint's. I got what I deserved all right."

His breath rattled in his throat. "Damnation." He grinned awfully. "Sorry, brother," he told Morgan. "See you in Hell."

Prospect shuddered massively and died.

Emma Franks came forward, oblivious to her cuffed wrists and the guns on her. "Weak as watered whiskey," she snapped. "Weak as every man of you."

Holt turned, fully intending to throttle her for her arrogance and craziness, for forcing him into a fight. It was Morgan who restrained him, and after some desultory struggling, Holt gave it up. "What a miserable goddamn way for this to end up," he said.

"No," Morgan said quietly in his ear. "You did well and you did right."

"And where exactly has that gotten me?" Holt snapped.

"Into a slightly better world, son," Pert offered. " 'Whatever a man soweth, that shall he also reap.' "

"Galatians, Chapter Six," Holt said automatically. He caught Sam smiling slightly.

"Very good, son." Pert prodded his new prisoner in the direction of Morgan's place, glanced up at the sky. "I'd warrant this storm is finally over," the marshal opined.

Chapter Twenty

"There are signs and there are signs," Holt said.

Sam gave him a sly look. "What's that mean?"

Holt made a sweeping gesture with his whole arm. "Consider the world around us. You'd almost think winter was over."

From his youth, Holt knew that chinooks usually came in January, but this season the phenomenon, warm northerly winds pushing bright days before them, had decided to arrive early. The sky was brilliantly clear, and the gusts in their faces were almost warm, sunlight and convection turning the snow beneath their horses' hooves to mush as they rode south along the broad Missouri River.

He should have felt less complacent, Holt thought, but no one could nurse morose notions in weather this fine. Still, Fort Benton and its telegraph, the line through which Pert could summon support that would put them both—or him at least—back behind bars could not be more than a few miles distant, and before they reached it some plan must be devised.

"Plans," Holt said aloud. "That's what I am supposed to be good at."

"Don't get ideas, son," Pert said. "I am—"

"Please don't say it, Marshal," Sam pleaded. "I'd sooner do a lifetime in the Federal penitentiary than be reminded that you are dogged."

Pert gave his attention to Emma Franks, who rode with her hands cuffed before her. Two days had passed since the business at Morgan's.

The wolfers took Pert's admonition to heart, and, near as anyone could tell, were gone from these parts. Morgan had made his peace with the Blackfeet, the few remaining wolves, and the land that had been returned to his stewardship without further threat.

They buried Prospect near the milky river. Charity wept, and when the makeshift ceremony was over, seemed changed. Before Pert rode them out, she took Holt aside. She was staying on with her uncle, she told him; here was a place and a time in her life to give up skittishness for industry—and for Fool's Eagle, with whom she'd become betrothed. Fool's Eagle shook Holt's hand, thanked him, and then stood in the background with his father, who scowled at his son's engagement more from habit than true ire. But the chief allowed himself a sly grin when Charity kissed Holt on the cheek in the course of good-byes.

"Quint was yellower than I thought," Emma said abruptly. "I should have known from way back then."

She was addressing Sam, as if it took a woman to understand what came next. "Back when?" Sam asked neutrally.

"We married in St. Louis, almost twenty years ago," Emma said. "Even in times when we were apart, I knew that he was needy of me."

Holt wondered how any man could need such a scrawny and plain specimen. He kept the thought to himself.

"He was a bully, but he got away with it," Emma said. "But then your redskin friend plunked out his jaw, not long before I caught up with him. He'd run out on me."

Emma reined up and trained her gaze on Sam. "You will understand."

Fort Benton turned out to be closer than Holt remembered. Now he could see the cluster of the town's buildings across the bench-land prairie, no more than a mile distant.

"Gutt rode south," Emma said to Sam. "That bit of information is the extent of my atonement."

Emma turned to Pert. "Will you shoot me in the back?"

Pert's eyes widened. "Don't even think about attempting escape."

"You won't," Emma decided.

Holt had never before seen Pert nonplussed, but he was now, as Emma spurred her horse and lit out at a full gallop, pressed close to the mane of her horse.

Holt crossed his hands on his saddle horn. "You're losing a prisoner, Marshal," he observed.

Pert looked at Emma's receding back.

"You got plenty of witnesses and a sure conviction. That's better than us." Holt looked at Sam. "Wouldn't you say?"

Pert was flustered. "You stay right on this spot. I will be back, and I expect to find you awaiting."

"Oh, we'll be here," Sam said airily.

"And if not, you must remember—"

Holt and Sam spoke simultaneously. "You are dogged."

Pert gazed desperately at Emma Franks, heading hell-bent for leather toward the horizon. "Got to apprehend that woman. Hope you apprehend Gutt." Pert sighed. "See you again—depend on it."

The marshal wheeled his horse and headed off after Emma. It was a good moment to make their own escape, Holt reckoned, but Sam seemed in no hurry. She watched Pert recede into the distance, her hand folded on her saddle horn. Time passed, while the sunlight grew warmer. After a while Pert disappeared from sight.

"That time in the mountains," Sam said.

"When we ran off on each other," Holt said. "I thought we talked that out."

"Night before that. I liked it."

Holt remembered: sleeping with her in his arms, close by and warm, gentling her shivers, and for that brief time immune from any storms that nature or the hand of man were brewing for them.

"Time to get going," he said roughly. "Which way?"

Sam wet a finger in her mouth, held it up to the slight breeze. "West?" she suggested.

Also by
Steven M. Krauzer

GOD'S COUNTRY

Wanted dead or alive, escaped convict Holt rode out into the rugged Utah territory to find the man who had framed him for the brutal murder of a mining camp madam. With his unlikely companion—the beautiful reporter, Samantha Lowell—Holt once again found himself fighting for justice on the wrong side of the law. Problem was, Holt had no trouble making enemies. And as bounty hunters, federal marshals, and gunslingers closed in, Holt knew the only way he was going to come out of this mess alive was with a loaded gun....

Published by Fawcett Books.
Available in your local bookstore.

Call toll free 1-800-733-3000 to order by phone and use your major credit card. Or use this coupon to order by mail.

__GOD'S COUNTRY   449-14868-8 $3.99

Name _____
Address _____
City_____ State_____ Zip _____

Please send me the FAWCETT BOOKS I have checked above.
I am enclosing $_____
 plus
Postage & handling* $_____
Sales tax (where applicable) $_____
Total amount enclosed $_____

*Add $2 for the first book and 50¢ for each additional book.

Send check or money order (no cash or CODs) to:
Fawcett Mail Sales, 400 Hahn Road, Westminster, MD 21157.

Prices and numbers subject to change without notice.
Valid in the U.S. only.
All orders subject to availability.   KRAUZER